*T*HE
ADVENTURES
❧ OF ❧
COUNTESS
VON SCHLEPPMEISTER

CONTAINS *THE JEWEL HEIST* & *THE CRUISE*

PREVIOUS BOOKS BY
ELISABETH von BERRINBERG

The City in Flames:
A Child's Recollection of World War II in Wurzburg, Germany

FORTHCOMING BOOKS BY
Elisabeth von BERRINBERG

The Cozy Connection, a cozy mystery series featuring

The Missing Madonna

A Culinary Experience

Mystery at the Pearly Gates

The Doppelganger.

THE
ADVENTURES
~ OF ~
COUNTESS
VON SCHLEPPMEISTER

CONTAINS *THE JEWEL HEIST* & *THE CRUISE*

ELISABETH VON BERRINBERG

BERRINBERG PUBLICATIONS
Minneapolis, Minnesota

ISBN: 978-0-9895915-2-2

Published by Berrinberg Publications, Minneapolis, MN

Cover and interior design by Jim Arneson,
Jaad Book Design, www.jaadbookdesign.com

Cover illustrations by Paula K Yff
www.paulayff.com

Ebook available from most online ebook sellers.

For information on obtaining interviews or permission for
excerpts, contact the author at lizvonb@q.com or Sybil Smith,
publisher@SmithHousePress.com.

FIRST EDITION

Berrinberg Publications, Minneapolis, MN

Printed in the United States of America

10 9 8 7 6 5 4 3 2 1

Dedication

*T*he Cozy Connection Mystery series is dedicated to the more than forty million senior citizen folks living in this country and about seventy-six million baby boomers.

While some of us may still enjoy reading hot and steamy romance novels, the romance in our own lives has somewhat lost its priority. Neither do we enjoy all that "gory stuff" in horror/thriller novels.

What we do like to read are those lightweight mysteries known as "cozies," preferably with the protagonist being one of us, such as some over-the-hill but otherwise likeable character who reminds us of ourselves. Or perhaps the old geezer whose dose of excitement derives from his "butting in" whenever his neighborhood turns into a crime scene. Or some little old lady whose "gut feeling" has never betrayed her when it comes to figuring out a "whodunit."

Such a person is the protagonist in my series.

So sit back with your favorite beverage and enjoy *The Adventures of Countess von Schleppmeister*, books one and two.

TABLE OF CONTENTS

TABLE OF CONTENTS

Book One

The
Jewel Heist

Book Two

The
Cruise

ACKNOWLEDGEMENTS

*M*y heartfelt gratitude is due to the many individuals who helped me persevere to the end of this endeavor:

Sybil Smith of Smith House Press Publishing Consultants, a patient and insightful mentor,

Doctors John and Joe Gindele for their thorough suggestions and expert testimonials,

James Arneson of Jaad for the book cover and interior design,

Paula Yff, for the clever cover illustrations,

Sissy and Sue Poettler for their excellent word processing skills,

Joe Dombeck for his diligent editing,

And Lorraine, Bernice, and Mary Jo, my test-readers who were kind enough to read my manuscripts.

BOOK ONE

$\mathscr{T}$HE
JEWEL HEIST

CHAPTER 1

*A*delheid von Schleppmeister stopped dead in her tracks. Her eyes on the ground, she followed footprints in the muddy path. Footprints that were not her own. Moving slowly, she followed them around her house, which had once been the servants' quarters and stable for the manor. But once she had reached the wooded area behind it, the trail of matted-down grass left by the intruder disappeared in the pine-needle covered ground of the forest.

At first she dismissed fears of someone stalking her. Instead, she attributed the footprints to one of her many visitors, the tourists who came to see the so-called Castle Morovia. In reality it was the Schenkenschloss—or, rather, the ruins of the Schenkenschloss—home of the ancestors of Count Otto von Schleppmeister, the now-deceased husband of Countess Adelheid von Schleppmeister. But then she remembered what Margarete had told her.

"They asked about you," she had said earlier that day, when Adelheid made her daily stop at the bakery to buy a piece of Margarete's apple strudel—the best in the region, as far as she was concerned.

Adelheid had not been too worried at the time. Tourists often asked the merchants along the main street of Hickelbrunn, a small town in the Austrian mountains, how to get to the road that led to the castle. Long ago, the castle had served as the location for a famous movie. They wanted to have their

3

picture taken in front of it. They often asked how it became a ruin. But Adelheid could not answer them. Not even Otto had known when she arrived there, many, many years ago, as his bride. She had often thought about it. It seemed like one of those stories she used to read, stories that usually began, "Once upon a time, quite long ago, there were kings and queens and counts and countesses who lived in old castles with winding stairs and secret passages and sometimes even ghosts."

There still are kings and queens, and some still live in castles. But in these modern times, they have adapted to modern lifestyles. Gone are carriages and knights in shining armor, with their stately horses. Now it's motorcars and airplanes that take them from one place to another. The descendants of such aristocrats are in no way living as their ancestors did, but they still enjoy the benefits of noble heritage. They may still live in castles, large or small, and they may still own some of the land that surrounds them.

In any case, they all have inherited their forefathers' titles, and thus they are thought of in their communities as being "was besseres"—in the eyes of ordinary folks, especially the poor people, they are of "a better kind."

Be that as it may, a title does not fill your purse or your bank account. And that fact was particularly noticeable for Adelheid who even by the standards of ordinary folks was, well, poor!

Having been a widow for quite some time now, Countess Adelheid von Schleppmeister was truly struggling to make a living. The Honorable (or was he really?) Count von Schleppmeister had been involved in some shady deals and had lost his fortune as a result. And because shady deals had gotten him into that mess, he hadn't dared go to the local authorities, for he might have ended up in the slammer himself.

Nobody ever knew the real reason why the countess preferred her old, rattling bicycle to convey herself. The town folks assumed that she could have very well been driving a car, and a better one at that. But her only income came from renting out a few acres of land to Franz Lohmeier, one of the local farmers, and selling postcards of her beloved Schenkenschloss during tourist season.

The postcards of the castle were aerial photographs and reproductions of paintings of the once stately home. The latter showed a time when horses grazed in the meadows and geese floated on the tiny pond that bordered a handsome structure built of natural stones. Those walls, long dilapidated, were now covered with damp moss and wild-growing plants.

The postcards also showed the "Brunnen," now rusty and forgotten, but with its hoist and bucket still in place. Tourists liked to pose before it, pretending to haul water from its now dried-up well.

Over the years, the countess found herself forced to sell off parcel after parcel of land, never letting on that it was out of desperation. Rather, she preferred to tell anyone who inquired about her reasons that she was just too old to carry on with maintaining large pieces of land. The few acres that surrounded the immediate estate had plum and apple trees and lots of raspberry bushes, and that, she said, was all the work she could handle.

Those who knew the countess were not always convinced by her explanations, and some were downright suspicious.

Surely anyone who watched this grand old lady, the way she swung herself onto her ever-present bicycle, would think she was in the prime of her life. True, her hair had long ago changed from a rusty, almost chestnut color to a dingy gray with only a hint of red left—a hint that was especially noticeable when the sunlight hit it at just the right angle. She was still quite youthful in her ways. Her gait was more like that of a woman in her mid-forties than of one whose last birthday cake featured two candles in the shape of a seven and a zero. However, few had the chance to observe that gait, for she was never without her bicycle, and she dismounted only when an incline in the road was too steep to manage astride her steel horse.

The countess stood about five feet, three inches tall; although there was a time when her passport indicated her height as five foot six, she was still of good build. In fact, she once was a triathlon athlete who had won medals and adulation.

It was during such an event that young Adelheid von Wehmhoffer met an equally young Otto von Schleppmeister who was not only handsome and athletic, but, by all accounts, also quite well-to-do. They felt a mutual attraction. She had eyes that seemed at times a translucent green and other times a rich hazel, which paired beautifully with her chestnut-red hair. He was a tall man with piercing brown eyes and brown hair that more often than not seemed to be begging for a trip to the local barbershop. His family owned the local lumber mill and the forest surrounding it.

This handsome youth had just emerged from some trying times. It was his brother, Johannes von Schleppmeister Jr., who had taken over the mill after the old count was killed by lightning one stormy night on his way home. Otto seemed to take it the hardest. But as time passed, and Otto was sent off to boarding school in Switzerland, he soon became his old self again. He loved sports, especially the competitive kind, and so it was that one day, on a whim, he decided to enter a regional triathlon competition with his school's team. That was a decision he never regretted. And even though his team scored poorly due to insufficient preparation on the part of certain participants, himself included, he scored big in another way instead. He won the heart of young Adelheid, and that prize was better than any medal or trophy he could have won.

But now Adelheid von Wehmhoffer, who was Countess von Schleppmeister, thought that her name was quite fitting, since she always seemed to be schlepping something. Usually in that oversized wicker basket permanently affixed to the back rack of her bicycle.

On her daily trips into town, she stopped at nearly all the shops along her path. There was the bakery, of course, with Margarete's incomparable apple strudel. One could not pass by that bakery when the aroma of cinnamon and other mouthwatering smells exuded from within.

So it was today, when the countess stopped in for her daily slice of that delicious apple strudel. There were strangers in the shop when she entered, as was often the case; tourists, attracted by the aroma of fresh-baked goods, often came in to buy some. Today there were four of them: two men, middle-aged as far as one could guess, and two women, probably their spouses. One of the women looked rather foreign. Her complexion was too dark to be a suntan, and her spoken words hinted of a language spoken in the Orient.

It was nothing out of the ordinary. Foreign tourists stopped in all the time to buy provisions for a hike into the nearby hills. But from what Adelheid could observe, there was no transaction in progress. Only conversation, and from what she picked up out of the swarm of words, those four strangers did not seem to be there to buy apple strudel or any other kind of pastry. They came for information, which of course was also not unusual, since the bakery was the first store from the highway on Main Street. There were no visible road signs, for Hickelbrunn was a town of, shall we say, minor significance. There was the Inn, but no hotels, and a tavern run by old Max Eisner, a man who, had anyone kept track of his birthdays, would probably need three candles: a one and two zeros.

So, Adelheid wondered, were these lost travelers stopping in for information on their whereabouts? Had they turned off the highway too soon? Or had they taken a left turn when they should have taken a right? It was definitely the case of the latter. The four strangers were turning left when they should have taken a right. A minor miscalculation... or was it?

Still deep in thought, the countess emerged from her daydreaming when she heard her name. "Guten Morgen, Countess! What will it be – the usual?"

The countess nodded, still a little startled by the sudden turning of heads. In unison, the four strangers turned away from the counter to gaze at Adelheid.

With an almost disappointed look, one of the women approached the countess and with equal disappointment in her voice exclaimed, "So, you are the Countess von Schleppmeister!" It sounded like she wanted to add, "Who would have thought that!" She quickly corrected herself by mumbling something presumably intended to be tactful, her disappointment was obvious. She turned toward one of the men and, shrugging her shoulders as if to say "You talk to her!" she stepped aside.

The countess had little patience with folks of that kind. The phonies, the pretenders, people who think they are better than you. They pretended to be of "good stock," as one would have said in the old days. But their true stock often shone through their demeanor. They might have money, but money does not give you class—social status perhaps, but not always class.

The woman behind the counter emerged to hand Adelheid a parcel. It was still warm to the touch, and she brought it up to her nose to enjoy a whiff of the aroma that wafted from the wrapping.

"Put it on my bill, Margarete," she called out as she turned and exited the store, not without returning a disapproving look to the woman who had spoken to her. *What an unpleasant person,* she thought as she opened the lid of her wicker basket to stow away her treat. Then, with a quick look back to assure herself that there was no oncoming traffic, she mounted her bike and leisurely pedaled down the street toward the butcher shop.

CHAPTER 2

*I*f Adelheid von Schleppmeister assumed that the encounter with that rude woman was the last she had seen of her, she was sadly mistaken. But aside from mentioning it to the butcher, she simply brushed it aside as just another tourist who didn't know better and soon forgot the incident. Perhaps, Adelheid thought, the woman's image of the aristocracy was what she had seen in those old-time movies. The lady of the house—pardon, the lady of the castle—sitting on her gilded settee, or was it a throne? Her delicate hands holding a device with a glowing cigarette at its end, more for show than for enjoyment. Servants buzzing about with trays of delicate china teacups to be gracefully offered to guests.

Well, this countess was indeed of a different sort. She was, as one would say, a down-to-earth person. Even in better days, she never felt that she was better than everyone else. Yes, there was a time when she could have driven a car, but night blindness had limited her range. Besides, whenever there was a need to travel abroad, it was the count who had done the chauffeuring. And whenever Otto was away on one of his many journeys, Adelheid had simply asked Philipp, the custodian of the estate, to take her to her destination. Philipp's mode of conveyance was not a motorcar, but rather an old, beat-up motorcycle, a Puch of Austrian make. Not too fast on the straight and narrow, but on a hill it had no trouble taking on a BMW of the same class.

Sometimes, when Philipp was too busy to take the countess on errands, he suggested that she drive it herself. "It's like a bicycle, only faster," he would joke. But the good old lady just didn't think that was such a good idea. She would rather put off her errands for another day.

Philipp was no longer officially in her employ, but he hadn't really left. She had told him that she didn't need help. After all, the few chores that needed to be performed on a daily basis were just enough to keep her busy. There were the chickens, three in all, and a rooster who, perhaps because of old age, was no longer able to fertilize the eggs—thus, none of them would ever hatch to increase the brood. At one time the chicken coop had held more than thirty chickens. But one by one they turned into chicken soup, or else met their demise by way of the fox that lived in the nearby forest.

The garden was small, about an acre or perhaps a bit more. The mature fruit trees needed no special care beyond some pruning once in a while. But Philipp insisted on doing it, not caring that he was not reimbursed for the work. Climbing ladders around trees, "Why, that's a man's job," he insisted.

There were also vegetables along the perimeter of the land: some carrots, tomatoes, even potatoes, albeit not enough to live off from crop to crop. Vines holding string beans climbed up the weathered wooden fence. And here and there some perennials returned faithfully each season to add color and fragrance in the otherwise austere place. It wasn't often that someone would wander beyond the walls of the castle to explore whatever was behind it, perhaps because (or especially because) one had to dodge chicken droppings and other debris.

But that was about to change. The forlorn and almost abandoned-looking spread would soon be visited by some very persistent and annoying guests, and the countess would not take kindly to their uninvited presence.

CHAPTER 3

"What did you think of the countess?" the woman asked her male companion. They had just settled into the local inn. Not as fancy as the hotel a few kilometers down the road in the next town, but with limited cash one has to be frugal.

"Oh, I think we can handle her," the man replied as he stripped his clothes to take a shower. The long drive down the country road had made itself visible in the form of layers of dust deposited on clothes and skin. *I will have to think of a way to approach her without arousing any suspicion, though,* he contemplated as he shut the shower door behind himself. Once he had adjusted the water to a comfortable temperature, he soaped himself down while singing in a loud but raspy voice the words of a famous opera. *"Ach wie so trügerisch,"* he belted out; then, almost whispering, he continued, *"sind Männerherzen."*

Had his female friend heard that last phrase, she might have gotten an inkling of what was in store for her. He sang of how deceitful men can be, though in the lyrics of the opera, it was the women who were deceitful.

But Maggie Lenz was too absorbed in herself to notice the change in words. And even if she had, one doubts that she would have known the difference. Her cultural education was limited, if it existed at all. Her background was nothing to brag about: a father who preferred to spend his time at the beer hall rather than at home with his family. A mother who, for reasons unknown, one day up and left, never to be heard from again.

So, with two young girls to take care of, Maggie's father had persuaded the newly divorced waitress from the beer hall to move in with him. "Because the girls need a mother," he insisted. Well, Maggie never did get along with her substitute mother, and one day, when she felt old enough to go out into the world on her own, she too just packed up and left. Her younger sister was the only one to know, but she promised not to tell where Maggie could be found.

Maggie had met a man at a street fest some time ago. Although he was somewhat older than her male peers, she took a liking to him. Before they parted she had told him her life story, how she was being treated by her father's mistress (as Maggie called her) and how she couldn't wait to get away from home and "see the world" someday.

"Come live with me," he had said. "I'll take care of you, Maggie girl." And Maggie, naive as she was, decided to accept his offer.

That was many years ago, in fact, more than she cared to remember. But then one day the police had come to take him away to prison. A witness had identified him as one of the men involved in a jewel heist. And so he had spent the last decade and a half in the slammer.

Maggie had promised to keep up the apartment, but soon what money she had called her own was gone. The rent was due, then late, and soon after that Maggie again found herself out on the street.

She managed to take on a job and even found a coworker who was willing to put her up. But living with another female was not nearly as exciting as living with a man. Men bought her clothes, they wined and dined her. Going out with the girls, it was Dutch treat every time.

Then one day, she happened to pass a kiosk where newspapers and periodicals were stacked up and weighed down with bricks, so as not to be blown away by the breeze. Her steady walk came suddenly to a halt before the newsstand. There, taking a few steps backward, she glanced—no, she stared—at the headline: "Tony Stengler soon to be paroled from prison" it screamed.

Quickly she gathered up some coins and handed the money to the vendor without even looking at him. Her eyes remained fixed to the paper now in her hands, and she continued her journey at a hurried pace.

The newspaper now folded under her arm, she unlocked the door to her apartment and, without taking off her coat, she settled into a stuffed chair that had seen better days.

She read the lead again: "Tony Stengler, the man who organized the famous Richtenberg jewel heist, will soon be a free man again!" It went on to explain that the jewels had never been recovered; police assumed that they had been smuggled out of the country and were probably stored at some rich sheikh's palace. Stengler, a one-time employee of an oil company, was known to have traveled to the Middle East on numerous occasions. Investigators concluded that on one such trip he had brought the jewels as well.

But where was the money? Surely he must have received a healthy sum for such precious loot. The insurance company claimed the value of eight and a half million schilling. His bank account showed no activity at the time, and the apartment he and Maggie had shared showed no signs of it either. On the contrary, the authorities found envelopes from the local bank lying unopened on the small commode in the entryway. Once opened, they contained only notices of overdrafts. Maggie herself had often wondered where the jewels or the money might be. She had been given the third degree by the law enforcement. But once they had realized that Maggie was not exactly the kind of person who could outwit the police, they just left her alone.

Maggie finally took off her coat, kicked off her high-heeled shoes, and again lowered herself into the chair to resume her reading. But soon she stopped. She just could not concentrate on the rest of the paper's contents. Her mind was on Tony Stengler. Should she contact the authorities to inquire about the exact date of Tony's release? Or should she just forget about the whole thing?

When Tony was sentenced and sent away, she had promised to visit him at least once a month. Soon a month became six weeks, then two months. And then, after arguing with Tony under the bored supervision of a guard, she just got up and left. She never went back. She had hoped to hear from Tony... for Tony to apologize to her for behaving like a jerk. But he too kept silent. So, as far as Maggie was concerned, life with Tony was history.

CHAPTER 4

*T*ony Stengler was a happy man. The parole board had, after many meetings, agreed to terminate his sentence, of which only a few months, eight to be exact, remained. Now he was free to collect the jewels that Otto had hidden for him.

I wonder how Otto is getting along, he thought. *Is he still alive? Or is he, too, locked up somewhere?*

He never heard any news that would confirm either. Tony figured that the old man was probably still sitting in his castle, watching over the loot that Tony had handed over to him to be hidden—preferably buried somewhere.

Otto von Schleppmeister, however, had never had a chance to watch over the buried treasure. The poor soul met his maker right around the time that Tony was arrested. In fact, it was not long after the local police had paid Otto a visit. They were looking for fugitives, they said. After asking many questions, they left. But Otto had known it wasn't over. *They'll be back!* he assured himself. The next morning Adelheid had found him slumped over his desk, a revolver still in his left hand. The physician and the coroner were sworn to secrecy as to the cause of the old gentleman's demise. Had anyone inquired, the answer was a simple, "It was his heart!"

Chapter 5

*A*fter signing out of Motel Delitto—Tony wasn't sure whether it meant "crime" or "criminal" in Italian, but either way it was a good name for his home of the last dozen or so years—he quickly made his way toward the railroad station.

"Hello, Tony!" came a voice from behind. Was he hearing things? Then again: "Tony, wait for me!" The voice came closer. He stopped to turn. A woman in high heels was trying to catch up with him.

"It's me, Maggie!" she called out. After reaching Tony, she breathlessly announced, "I have been waiting for you, Tony!" She reached out to embrace him, but Tony grabbed her arms and just held on to them. "Really!"

Tony laughed. "Did you really wait for me all this time?" he asked with a hint of sarcasm in his voice.

"No, silly!" she chuckled. "I have been waiting for you at the gate, but you must have slipped right by me."

Maggie didn't have the nerve to tell him that she was awaiting a man with handsome features and the build to match it. It wasn't until the last person had passed through the gate that she noticed in the distance a man walking somewhat slower than the rest of them, his left leg hinting at a slight limp. It was him, Tony. She had forgotten about his handicap. A souvenir from an accident, he had once explained to her. What Maggie saw now was a man whose once raven-black hair was speckled with gray. His athletic build had changed into a floppy, belly-protruding slump, and his eyes were covered with spectacles that gave him a completely different look.

"How have you been, Maggie-girl?" he asked, not really interested in an answer. But she was here now, and even though he had not yet figured out what his next move might be, he decided to play along.

The list of places of employment that the warden had handed out was in his pocket. But Tony had no plans to pursue any of them. His mind was elsewhere: the jewels! The loot buried somewhere on the grounds of an old castle in Austria. His retirement fund.

Otto von Schleppmeister, his noble friend, had offered to bury them. To be sure of finding them again, he had made a drawing of the castle grounds that Tony had kept hidden. Likewise, Otto had kept a copy of the drawing hidden in his study. But then a witness to the crime had led the police to Tony Stengler, whom he recognized as a former classmate. Tony's accomplice, the getaway driver, never did get caught. Even Tony barely knew the man, Ludwig Heimler, whom he had met only shortly before the heist. All he knew was that Heimler had once worked as a farmhand and had a wife who came from somewhere in the Middle East.

Tony had to find the castle. He had to get his hands on those jewels. Tony had met the count at a casino some time earlier. In spite of the fact that Otto was quite a bit older, they had become friends, for Tony had charisma. Never one to be intimidated by folks with titles or rank, Tony was a breath of fresh air in Otto's life. Count Otto von Schleppmeister, one of the pillars of the community, preferred the company of plain folks to that of people whose main desire was to be seen in the company of a real count. That in itself makes good material for gossip—well , at least it did back then.

But here and now, Tony was determined to seek out the castle and dig up his much-desired fortune.

CHAPTER 6

*W*hen Tony left the prison, Maggie wasn't the only one waiting for his release. Off to the side of the gate stood a man and a woman, inconspicuously examining everyone who passed through the iron gate.

They too had almost missed him. Then, when Maggie had called out to Tony, they knew they had found who they were looking for.

"How do you suppose we should go about this?" the woman asked her companion. "I mean, not letting on that we are here, when you need to make contact with him?"

"Let's not worry about that just yet!" the man said. "Right now all I need to know is where he is going, where he's going to stay, and what his plans are from here on. And you, *dear*, are going to help me!" he concluded, looking sheepishly at his spouse.

Ludwig Heimler, a man of medium stature, had been married for many years. They never had any children. Soraya's complexion and accent reflected her homeland in the Middle East. Her age was hard to define: she had no lines or other age-revealing signs, and at times one could have thought them to be father and daughter.

CHAPTER 7

"Where do you live, Maggie-girl?" Tony inquired. He had some thoughts about why Maggie had come all the way to Salzburg to pick him up from prison.

"Well," she began hesitantly, "it's like this: I have a roommate, you see." She paused, anticipating that he might want to move in with her.

"Is it a man?" Tony wanted to know.

"Oh no, Tony!" she quickly answered. "It's a woman! We work together," she added.

Tony tipped his head to the side and looked straight at Maggie.

"Would there be room for me?" he asked with a smile.

Maggie was not ready to answer. Should she tell him that she lived with someone else out of necessity? That she couldn't afford to rent an apartment on her own? The wages she earned from her employment were just enough to pay her share of the rent, and there were times when there was just enough money left to buy food. She was at the mercy of Anita Sprenger, who, after having worked at Neckermann's department store for nearly thirty years, had the most seniority of all forty-two employees and a salary to match it. She had occupied that apartment for nearly as long—twenty-eight years, to be exact. Furthermore, it was only minutes away from Neckermann's, so Anita had neither reason nor desire to move, even though by now she could have afforded to live in a better neighborhood.

Finally, Maggie answered, "Tony, I'm not sure how to say this, but my roommate is…it's her apartment, you see. Anita… I mean, Fräulein Sprenger, does not believe in couples living together without the benefits of matrimony."

So that's where this is going! Tony suddenly realized. *She wants to get married. Get married to good old Tony. The soon-to-be-rich Tony!* No sign of her, no letters or phone calls to Motel Delitto for nearly fourteen years, and then on his day of freedom, there she was: "Hello Tony! It's me, Maggie!"

Tony shook his head, still absorbed in his thought. Then he looked at Maggie. "Let her move somewhere else," he was about to say, when another thought came to his mind. But not being able to speak about it just then, he instead nodded and went on. "Is there a *pension* near your place?" After getting an affirmative answer, he just said, "Okay, let's get on our way!"

CHAPTER 8

"*E*xcuse me, Madame, for being so inquisitive, but I think I just saw an old friend entering your establishment, one whom I would like to very much see again!"

The woman behind the old wooden desk at Pension Luger did not look up; she kept on filing papers into an old-fashioned binder as she answered, "Ye-e-es?" with a deliberate stretch that seemed to say, "And what do you want me to do about it?"

Without waiting for an answer, she continued, "Room seventeen, second door to the right!"

"Well, you see," Ludwig Heimler said, a little startled, "I… I *do* want to make sure it was him before I go, you see, I have not seen him for many years, and it would be embarrassing if I were to knock on his door and it wasn't him."

The woman finally looked up. Her piercing eyes met his. "Name?" she demanded.

Unprepared for such an inquisition, he had to improvise. Off to his left was the door to the elevator. Above it was a metal plate emblazoned with "Otis" and beneath it, in small letters, "elevator manufacturer."

"Oh! Ah, my name is Otis, Karl Otis," Ludwig lied.

The woman looked impatient. "No! I mean the name— what is the name of your friend?"

"Oh, it's Stengler, Tony Stengler!" Ludwig replied. Without checking her logbook, the woman asked, "Should I let him know you are here?"

"Oh no!" Ludwig blurted out. "You see, I want it to be a surprise, and I would just as soon that you not tell him that I'm here. I'll wait 'til tomorrow to pay him a visit. He'll still be here, won't he?" He had to be sure.

"For the rest of the week," she volunteered as she glanced at the logbook in front of her.

CHAPTER 9

"*T*hat was close!" Ludwig laughed as they left the pension. He and Soraya walked quickly now to seek out their own quarters for the night. Ludwig had accomplished what he had come for: *Tony is using his own name rather than registering with a fictitious one.*

"He must not suspect anything!" he chuckled as he sat down on his bed. He kicked off his shoes and then, with a long sigh, lowered himself onto the oversized down pillow.

Soraya had not spoken a lot during their walk back. But she was curious all the same.

"So what's your next move?" she asked as she sat down on the bed next to his.

"Let's talk about it tomorrow," he answered with a yawn. "It's been a long day!"

Soraya had to be satisfied with his answer, at least for now. But she was eager to find out just what he had meant by his earlier remark about her "helping" him.

CHAPTER 10

*A*s Adelheid von Schleppmeister once again was on her daily shopping trip, she, as usual, stopped at Margarete's Bakery first.

"Oh, Countess!" Margarete exclaimed, "Am I ever glad to see you! I've... eh, I've been a little worried about you!"

"Why would you be worried about me, Margarete?" the countess replied.

"Those people," Margarete continued, "those strangers." She paused. Should she tell the countess what she had overheard?

"What about those strangers?" Adelheid now wondered. She still remembered her unpleasant encounter with them—the disrespectful demeanor of one of the women.

Margarete, still fidgeting with the apple strudel she was wrapping up for Adelheid, now stopped and looked up. "They were asking about you!" she blurted out. "They wanted to know where your—your—'castle' was located and who else lived there!"

"My castle?" Adelheid laughed. "So they wanted to know where my—*ahem*—castle was located?" She shook her head in amazement. "What exactly did you tell them, Margarete?"

"Well," Margarete began, "I told them that there were only the ruins of a castle and a building of some sort."

"A stable!" the countess corrected her.

"And that you live..." she paused. "Where exactly do you live, Countess?" the baker-woman wanted to know.

33

Adelheid was a little surprised at Margarete's inquiry. She had assumed that it was common knowledge in the community that she lived in the converted stable. And that the castle, if it could ever have been called a castle, had fallen into disrepair and, as rumors had it, that it was haunted.

"Thank you, Margarete, for your concern." Adelheid extended her hand to touch Margarete's shoulder. "I'll be all right, but thank you again for telling me."

With that, Adelheid left the store to continue with her errands. If there was any concern on her mind, she certainly didn't show it. She thought back to the day of the incident, the encounter with those strangers. She tried to remember their faces. She had no trouble remembering the woman who addressed her, bad-mannered as she was. But the others? She just had not paid that much attention to them at the time. This being a region with beautiful mountains off in the distance and forest as far as one could see, it was no wonder that tourists flocked to the area to hike.

When Adelheid arrived at home, she deposited her bicycle in its usual place. But then, after a moment of hesitation, she returned and wheeled it a few feet away to a toolshed that had just enough space left to keep it out of sight. A little push was all it took to shut the door behind it.

CHAPTER 11

"*L*ook, baby!" Soraya began as she sat at a small table, still in her dressing gown, an ashtray in front of her and a cigarette in her mouth, "Why don't we just confront them, tell them that you have a right to a share of the jewels, maybe not an equal share, but at least some!"

"I know I can't claim a big share," Ludwig conceded. "After all, I did not have to spend umpteen years in the slammer. But I will certainly try. And besides, I know the spot where the jewels are buried, so Tony needs me!" he said triumphantly.

But Soraya knew better.

"If you know so much, then how come you never went after them all this time?"

"Well... They are buried on the castle grounds, I know that much!"

"Yes, Ludwig, but remember what the woman in the bake shop said. 'There is *no* castle!'"

Impatient, Ludwig snapped at her, "Put out that stinking cigarette and let's figure out our next move. First, we've got to decide how to arrange our, ah, *meeting* with Tony and his woman. And then we can go from there."

CHAPTER 12

*I*t was easier than Ludwig had anticipated, though not at all as he had planned. Making contact with Tony Stengler simply happened through circumstances that were far better than any imaginative plan.

The restaurant, not far from the pension where Tony and Maggie had put up for the night, was quickly filling up with dinner guests. When the couple joined the line at the entrance, the hostess assured everyone that it would be only a few minutes before another table was cleared. When she finally called Tony and Maggie to follow her, she led them to a table already occupied by two other guests, a man and a woman. Sharing a table with other guests was customary in Europe, so they saw nothing unusual about it.

What *was* unusual, however—or at least it seemed so to the hostess—was the startled reactions of the two men.

Ludwig had not changed a lot in his appearance over the years. But Tony had. Ludwig wondered, should he pretend not to recognize Tony? After all, without Maggie's shouted greeting at the prison gate, Tony surely would have slipped by him, never to be seen again.

"Heimler?" Tony asked the man across from him as he dropped into his chair.

"Yes, I am Heimler," Ludwig answered, not really knowing just yet how to behave.

"And who might you be? Have we met?"

"It's Tony, Tony Stengler. Remember me?"

Ludwig could have won an acting award for the next scene.
"Tony, my man! How are you? How nice to see you again!"
he went on. And then, uncertain about how to broach the
subject of Tony's imprisonment when he himself had gone
free, Ludwig just waved to the server. "Herr Ober! Some wine
please!" And then to Tony, "Let's celebrate our reunion with
a glass of wine, shall we?"

CHAPTER 13

*A*fter sitting in the restaurant for nearly three hours, Tony and Ludwig were still talking. The two women showed no particular interest in their conversation.

"So, how long have you and Ludwig been married?" Maggie asked Soraya. Not that she really cared to know, but at least she might be able to establish what sort of loyalty existed between the two. If Soraya was just an acquaintance, she might not be aware of Ludwig's past. Maggie herself had only heard Ludwig's name mentioned occasionally when Tony, before his arrest, was having frequent "meetings" with friends, as he had explained his sometime extended absences.

Soraya was not sure how much information she should reveal to a woman she had just met. Ludwig had told her that Tony had a girlfriend at the time of his arrest, but he was not sure what became of her after their forced separation. Did she know about the whereabouts of the jewels? If she did, surely she wouldn't be sitting here right now. She would have found a way to get hold of them and then live a life of leisure in some faraway place.

"Oh," Soraya began slowly, "Ludwig and I have been married for nearly ten years now." She had met him at an outing where she and some friends had put up a tent to settle in for the night. Ludwig was working in a field nearby. It was harvest time, and he had hired on for the season. Once the crop was stored away, he planned to pack up and leave, not knowing where he would end up.

But on one of those days in the field, he saw a group of young women pitching a tent at the edge of the field. He wandered toward them, intending to inform them that this was private property and they would have to settle down elsewhere. But it never came to that.

He could only see a girl with the darkest eyes he'd ever encountered. Her skin was the color of bronze, and her smile revealed a mouthful of teeth that seemed even whiter against her deep complexion.

She was a foreigner who had come to Austria to study. But she, too, was smitten. Ludwig's suntanned body, as he stood there shirtless, revealed strength and a certain kind of sex appeal in spite of his windblown hair and sweaty face, from which he wiped pearls of perspiration with a handkerchief long overdue for laundering.

"Yes, we met and fell in love," she continued. And though Soraya had come from a land of different customs and traditions, where marriages were arranged, she had made up her mind, against all protests by her family, to share the rest of her life with Ludwig.

They both were restless souls, never able to stay in one place for too long. They once even joined the circus, Soraya as the Mädchen für Alles, a person whose job was to fill in wherever needed. Mostly she had helped by preparing meals for the performers or mending their costumes when they needed repair. Once she even had to fill in for an assistant to a sword-swallower. But that was just too much for Soraya to handle. The sight of that long piece of metal disappearing into the.... No, there was no way she was going to stand by and watch. She had to leave. So without ever finishing her debut as a circus performer, she dropped the prop she was holding and staggered toward the exit, where her stomach relieved itself of its contents.

It wasn't too long after that when they had both decided that they'd had enough of life with the circus and so went on to new endeavors.

into the... No, there was no way she was going to stand by
and watch. She had to leave. So without ever finishing her
debut as a circus performer she dropped the prop she was
holding and staggered toward the exit, where her stomach
relieved itself of its contents.

It wasn't too long after that when they had both decided
that they'd had enough of life with the circus and so went
on to new endeavors.

CHAPTER 14

*W*eeks had passed since Tony and Ludwig's reunion. They had decided to pursue their treasure hunt together. Neither knew of the other's true intentions. Could they trust each other? Who would find the jewels first? Before they could even begin their search, though, they had to seek out the count, the pal and confidant who had willingly offered to hide the loot after the heist.

It was big news back then, all over Europe. "Jewel robbers take loot by posing as security guards," the headlines had read.

They knew that Otto could be trusted, for he too had a streak of larceny running through his blue-blooded veins. Count or no count, Otto was a gambler, and gamblers know no bounds at times. As Otto got himself deeper and deeper into debt, he resorted in desperation to means that were not always honorable. Cheating at card games was one of his vices, but that ended once his card-playing partners were onto him.

When Otto met Tony Stengler, they were both sitting at a casino table where a roulette wheel spun around and around, determining who had just lost a fortune and who had suddenly become rich. But Lady Luck never was on either man's side. Soon they had plotted a scheme that meant they would never have to worry about money again.

Earlier, Tony had met a man who was in need of employment after leaving the circus. He had decided to promise the man a job, albeit with a warning that it might involve unpleasant consequences. But Ludwig Heimler was nearly broke by then, for he and Soraya found no work after leaving the circus. They had used up their meager savings and were about to be kicked out of their furnished apartment, if one could call it that. A room with a bed and a couch, a kitchen too tiny to move around in when more than one person occupied it. The bathroom was down the hallway and shared with two other tenants. The window was devoid of curtains, and at night they hung a bed sheet to ensure privacy.

But the rent was cheap, and the landlady, a retired schoolteacher, was more than accommodating whenever the rent wasn't paid on time. However, with the rent unpaid for nearly three months and the first of the month approaching, the landlady had finally insisted on getting some money. "Pay up, or you must leave!" she ordered.

So it was that the following night, once the landlady was sound asleep, Ludwig and Soraya packed their bags and quietly, with shoes in hand, left the premises and disappeared into the night.

The note they left behind read, "Please forgive us for leaving like this, but we'll pay you soon, that's a promise."

That promise was never kept, even though Ludwig had honestly intended to pay the lady once he got hold of the share Tony had promised him. Instead, his share and the rest of it ended up buried at some old castle, its whereabouts unknown to him.

CHAPTER 15

*E*verything went so fast back then. The car Ludwig was supposed to drive away, once Tony had gotten hold of the jewels, was a rental that Tony had signed for under a phony name and phony identification as well.

They were to drive into the country, away from the city where the heist had taken place. This scenario went partially as planned. They *did* make it out of the city, and they *did* drive some distance. In fact, they were nearly at their destination, where Otto was waiting to hide their loot.

Neither Tony nor Ludwig had bothered to check the gasoline gauge, which showed the needle pointing near empty. And empty it was. After driving for a good hour, they came to realize their oversight. They knew that stopping at a gas station was too risky, for the news of the robbery was surely all over the wires by that time. So they decided to walk the rest of the way.

They heard sirens in the distance. Were the police after them? But they were looking for a car, not hikers. The car, however, would be found soon, they were sure, and it was a lead to which direction the thieves had taken. They had pushed it into a small path off the main road where some overgrown shrubs kept it out of sight.

The sirens came closer. It was beginning to rain, and lightning streaked across the evening sky. Thunder followed, and with it the rain turned into a downpour.

"Let's split up!" Tony suggested, deciding that those sirens were out to get them. The headlights of a car became visible in the distance, and the blue strobe lights atop its roof convinced the men that it was time to separate.

Tony had disposed of the small case that held the jewels and poured them into a nondescript canvas bag. Weight in carats does not compare with the weight in pounds, so Tony had no problem climbing up a hill where a stretch of forest would soon swallow him up.

Ludwig remained on the country road. He had removed his jacket, which he tossed over his shoulder, and noticing farm implements up ahead, he came up with a plan.

The gendarmes were coming nearer. The steep hill required them to shift into a lower gear. Ludwig had just enough time to reach the farm tractor, and he crawled beneath it until he was out of sight. Should they stop to search and find him, "I'm just staying out of the rain" would be enough to convince them that he was not who they were looking for. With his experience as a farmhand, he would have no trouble answering questions about the tractor, should they inquire.

The sirens stopped, and so did Ludwig's heart. Well, almost. *They are here!* he realized. *They know where to look for me!* He anticipated being pulled from his hiding place to be put in handcuffs and led away. Well, it never happened.

Instead he heard a car shifting into another gear, then again, and once more. Suddenly, he realized that the car had shifted into reverse, then forward, and again in reverse, then forward once more to speed away in the direction from whence it had come. The narrow country road made it hard to manage a U-turn without leaving the solid surface of the road. Had it reached the black soil of the freshly tilled field, it surely would have gotten stuck in the now rain-soaked earth.

Ludwig couldn't even bear to think of the outcome. Would he have tried to run, had they found him? With their vehicle no longer useful to them, they would have had to pursue him on foot. But no! They would have just shot him, he was certain of that.

He shuddered just thinking of it. But instead they had left. They never *did* get stuck, and best of all, they never *did* find him.

Ludwig decided to wait out the storm. The tractor was not too much of a shelter, and open spaces left water dripping from above. He soon was soaked, his clothes not only wet, but full of mud as well.

The storm finally passed over. Lightning was still visible in the distant night sky, but the thunder was now only a deep rumble somewhere beyond. Ludwig emerged from his hideout. It was useless to try and remove the soil that now covered pretty much all of his clothes, for it would only have worsened it.

He turned to look off into the stretch of wooded land where he had last seen Tony disappear. He thought, *Should I go back to find him, so we can continue our journey together? Or should I try and find the castle on my own and meet up with Tony there? It could not be too far from here!* But in the dark, wet and dirty as he was, there was not much else he could do.

After Ludwig had left the road and wandered into the woods, hoping to find Tony waiting to continue by daylight the next morning, he did not get too far. The underbrush was just too much for him. He returned to the edge of the forest and, with his jacket serving as a pillow, he lowered himself to the ground to wait out the night. The sky had become quiet—almost eerily quiet. The rain had stopped, and aside from the sound of a twig breaking loose from a branch, not much else was audible. He kept listening intensely, hoping to hear footsteps within the dense brush around him to indicate that Tony had returned from wherever he was hiding. But to no avail. The only new noise was that of his growling stomach. How long since he last ate? He tried to count the hours that had passed. Then he tried to concentrate on his next move. Should he just forget about the whole affair? Pretend it never happened and return to Soraya, who by now must be worried sick? Sleep was out of the question. He had to stay awake so that he could hear it, should Tony pass by. But hungry and tired as he was, sleep won him over; his unresisting eyes fell shut, and off he was to dreamland.

CHAPTER 16

*T*ony also planned to wait out pursuit by the long arm of the law. A small stretch into the thicket he had spotted a deer stand, a pedestal in a tree used by hunters as a lookout for wild game. With some effort, he had reached the wide wooden seat at the top. On its side was a small shelf, presumably used to hold a weapon and "proviant," evidence of which remained: a sandwich, abandoned by a hunter who might have left in a hurry as the storm approached. Or left there for the wild birds to feast on once he had satisfied his own hunger. The wrapping had given some protection, for part of its contents was still dry.

Without hesitation, Tony discarded the rain-soaked part of his find and, with the appetite of a man used to large portions, devoured the meager grub before him, salami and cheese on hearty rye bread.

Before Tony had reached the deer stand, he had heard the car passing below. The sirens were now silent, and shifting gears rang in his ears. He didn't pay much attention, for shifting was frequent on a hilly road such as the one below. So he never guessed that the police car had turned around and, for all intents and purposes, given up the pursuit. Via police radio, the driver and his partner had been informed that the getaway car had been found in the vicinity of the town of Hickelbrunn, and thus the search would concentrate on that area.

Tony decided to wait until dawn before he resumed his journey. He had planned in earnest to find Ludwig so they could reach the castle together. But the urgency of finding Ludwig soon gave way to other plans. If Ludwig reached the castle before him, then so be it. But if Ludwig had decided to return to the city, Tony would not make any effort to find him.

CHAPTER 17

$\mathcal{L}$ udwig had indeed decided to return to the city. After he awoke from his most unusual resting place, he quickly headed for the road below, passing the tractor that had been his refuge earlier. He walked until he saw, off in the distance, a watering station for farm animals. A well beneath it brought spring water to its top. Ludwig looked around. There was no one in sight. It was still too early in the morning for anyone to be out. Not even the local farmers, early risers as they were known to be, had appeared to resume their work in the fields. After the last night's storm, the ground would not be workable until the sun had dried it out. So today the farmers would have to stay home to pursue other chores.

Ludwig could now leisurely rid himself of his muddy coating and give his clothes a quick laundering in the trough. With one more look around to assure himself of his solitude, he stripped the last piece of clothing and submerged himself in the tub. The water was cold, and shivers came over him. He washed off the mud, then gave his hair a quick rinse under the makeshift faucet. When Ludwig reached for the pump to increase the flow from its usual trickle, he received an icy shower that made his teeth chatter.

The sun rose quickly and a morning breeze, although not kind to his unclothed body, speeded his laundry on its way to dryness. *Thank heaven for drip-dry garments,* he thought. His lightweight trousers and cotton shirt were soon dry enough to be worn again. He stuffed his socks into his windbreaker. His sandals were still damp, but between the breeze around him and the warmth of his feet, they too would soon be dry again. It was time to leave.

Judging by the steady hum of engines and the occasional wail of what was, unmistakably, the horn of an eighteen-wheeler, he was only minutes away from the highway. Once there, he planned to flag down the driver of one such freight car, for truckers often welcomed the company of hitchhikers, if only because conversation helped them stay alert.

Only two trucks had passed before a third one shifted down at the sight of Ludwig's extended hand.

"Where you headed?" the driver asked as he stuck his head out of the cab.

"Ried!" Ludwig hollered over the roar of the engine. With a nod of his head, the driver motioned for Ludwig to climb up the footboard, where he swung open the door and settled down for the journey ahead.

Had Ludwig been a religious man, a prayer would have been due to his maker. He had escaped the law. Had survived a cold and wet night in the boondocks, the Hinterland, as Soraya would call it. He had even overcome the hunger he had felt earlier. The well water had filled his stomach enough to at least keep it from rumbling.

The driver did not speak a lot, and Ludwig was glad. He was not in the mood to carry on a conversation with a stranger. Although he was grateful for the ride, he was glad when the first outskirts of the city came into sight.

"You can drop me off by the next streetcar stop," he offered.

The driver shifted down and slowly came to a halt.

"Thanks again, and have a nice day!" he said, waving at the driver while dismounting the cabin.

The driver just nodded and, with a quick glance at his rearview mirror, pulled away, shifting gears until he had rejoined the steady stream of cars and trucks that hurried past.

A minute later a trolley turned the corner and stopped to pick up a passenger. Ludwig was on his way home

CHAPTER 18

*N*early two hours had passed since Tony emerged from the woods. He had wandered in what he thought to be the direction of the castle. He had seen it only once before, and that from a distance. The turret that protruded from its ancient walls was the first structure one could see from afar. But no matter how hard Tony peered into the distance, there was no tower anywhere in sight.

A car rumbled down the road as Tony watched, careful not to be seen. But then, when the car was almost upon him, he leaped from behind the tree that had hidden him. With both arms vigorously waving to signal the driver to stop, he yelled out, "Otto!" and then again, "Otto, over here!"

Although Otto's journey had no purpose other than searching for Tony and his accomplice, he was not expecting to run into Tony so soon. He had heard the news of the robbery over the wires the night before. According to Tony's plan, they were to meet Otto at the castle to stash the loot until it was safe to turn it into cash.

Otto had heard that a car, presumed to be the getaway car, had been found in the woods near Hickelbrunn. He knew that his buddies could not be far way. Fearing that he would be implicated, should they appear on his property, he had thought it best that they never reach the castle. Instead, he had set out in search of them, to take the jewels and carry on as planned.

"They are after you!" he greeted Tony as he cranked down the car window. "We mustn't be seen together," he continued in an urgent voice, glancing at his rearview mirror to reassure himself that no one was following him. But his worries were unfounded, and after regaining his composure, he turned off the engine.

"Is this the stuff?" he asked, pointing at the bag in Tony's hands. Tony confirmed with a nod of his head.

"Get in!" Otto ordered.

Quickly, the thief followed his command. *He must think he is still in the Kaiser's Army*, Tony thought. Of course, while the old man was old enough to be his father, the count certainly hadn't been around when the land was ruled by kings and emperors.

"Get down!" Otto ordered as he started up the car again. And not a minute too soon.

Coming around the bend in the road was a farmer, on foot. Realizing that the farmer had probably recognized him—who wouldn't know the old Count Otto von Schleppmeister around these parts?—Otto grudgingly slowed down again. He pulled a blanket off of the passenger seat and threw it into the back, hissing, "Cover up, quickly!" as the man came nearer.

"Guten Morgen, Herr Graf!" the farmer greeted him while doffing a weathered hat. Otto resigned himself to stopping for a chat, as was customary in these parts, so as not to arouse suspicion by rushing away.

"How is the missus?" he asked politely, though at this particular moment, he couldn't have cared less about the farm wife's well-being. He was too worried about his passenger giving him away.

"That was quite a storm we had last night!" the farmer remarked as he replaced his hat on his head.

"Yes, indeed!" Otto agreed, "that's why I'm out here. Had to check on some trees that might have gotten damaged during the storm." *What an excuse for being seen out here!* he thought to himself. At least the farmer wouldn't be wondering why the count was up and about at such an early hour.

After exchanging a few more pleasantries, Otto felt safe in excusing himself and continuing down the road. Soon the farmer was far enough away for Otto to signal all-clear to his passenger.

Tony emerged, his nose dripping and his eyes watering. The blanket had recently served as a bed for one of the castle's other inhabitants, a cat who had decided to drop her litter on the passenger seat of Otto's car.

"I need some air!" Tony gasped. "Open the windows, please!" He sneezed again and again, "Hatchoo!" crying "Oh what an ordeal!" between sneezes.

Otto was glad to comply. He shuddered to think of the consequences had Tony been unable to hold back the urge to sneeze. He could see the headlines right now: "Count so-and-so implicated in jewel robbery!"

They had reached a fork in the road. The castle, or rather, the remains of it, was to the right; the left fork led to the main highway.

"You have to leave now," the count began, unsure of what Tony's reaction might be. He slowly continued, "I cannot let you be seen with me. Go back to the city, and I will get in touch with you as soon as possible!"

Tony, by now too tired and hungry to care, got out of the car without a word, but with one last glance at the bag beside him. His right hand stroked that precious parcel one last time. Otto reached into his coat pocket and then handed Tony a piece of paper.

"Here!" he began in a subdued voice. "This is a diagram of the castle grounds. I will mark the spot—the grave," he added with a forced smile, "with a marker and a pile of stones. I'll mail you the details."

Tony merely nodded, and with a wave of his hand he was on his way. *If all goes well, he shall soon become a rich man,* he mused as he proceeded toward the main road, where he was soon swallowed up by the never-ending traffic.

CHAPTER 19

*W*hen Count Otto arrived back at the estate, Adelheid was waiting for him. With a concerned look, she inquired, "Where have you been, Otto?" It was unusual for Otto to be up and about before her. He was a late sleeper. But today he had hoped to leave before his departure was noticed. Otto remained calm.

"Didn't you hear the storm last night?" he asked, knowing full well that she had. He had heard her as she returned from the yard, having secured the shutters on the windows facing the approaching storm.

"Of course I heard the storm!" she laughed, and with a wave toward their quarters she added, "Come, your breakfast is getting cold!" Otto gladly followed her suggestion.

Adelheid had long ago given up inquiring about her husband's whereabouts. She never could get an honest answer anyway. She let him believe that she accepted his stories and excuses, but she knew better. She was just too old and too tired to pursue his escapades any further.

Later that night, Otto set out to complete his mission. He had at first planned to bury the bag, jewels and all. There were ladies' rings studded with emeralds and rubies, bracelets of gold and silver, and then the crème de la crème—the necklace! By some accounts it had once been in the possession of the Tsarina of Russia.

Keeping the box in his safe would have been too risky, for Adelheid would have soon discovered it. But the strongbox from the safe was not too large. He could easily carry it to his car without being noticed. The canvas pouch with the jewels still lay partially hidden under the cat blanket in the car. Quickly he transferred its contents into the metal box and wrapped the pouch around it.

It was dark enough that Adelheid could not see him, should she be watching from a window. After one quick stop by the toolshed, where a shovel was waiting, he proceeded to the back of the stable. Hastily he began to dig. He stopped, thinking he had heard some noise, but there was no sign of anybody and he continued to dig.

"Otto! Are you out there?" Adelheid's voice rang through the still of the night. Then she hollered again, "Otto! Are you all right?"

"I'm back here, Adelheid!" he answered. He had just finished the deed when Adelheid first called out. The strongbox was buried and out of sight, but the canvas pouch lay beside him.

He swiftly picked it up and tossed it behind a woodpile just before his wife rounded the corner.

"What are you doing back here?" Adelheid demanded.

The shovel in Otto's hands was enough to convince her that he had just chased away the old fox who had come looking for his supper, another one of Adelheid's chickens.

No, he could never let Adelheid find all this. Besides, he already had told his cohorts where to find the loot.

CHAPTER 20

The canvas pouch now hung on a rusty nail in the toolshed, where it held Adelheid's garden tools. Pruning shears and the like protruded from a hole in the fabric. It was showing its age, as it had been exposed to sun and rain over the years, fourteen to be exact. Adelheid had found it one day, tucked in a pile of wooden logs that had been stacked behind the stable, to be used in the fireplace on cold winter nights. The otherwise sufficient heating system was just not enough to handle the worst of the cold.

At first, Adelheid had thought it to be Philipp's property, which he had purposely left out for carrying logs to the quarters. But once he had assured her that he had never seen it before, she figured that a tourist must have left it there. When nobody came to claim it, she decided to put it to use. Once gardening season passed, it hung in the rafters of the shed along with the other gardening miscellany.

CHAPTER 21

The day had come. Tony and Ludwig's recovery scheme was to become reality. They had spent many hours together, trying to recall the name of the town through which they passed before their rented car left them stranded.

Now Tony opened an atlas in front of him. With a loupe pressed to his eye, he traced the area he thought to be the place where they had parted.

"Hickelhausen, Hickelstadt, Hickelsomething?" Ludwig tried to remember. "Hickelbrunn?" Tony asked, his finger pressed down on the map so as not to lose the spot where he had just read the name.

"Yeah! That's it! Hickelbrunn!" Ludwig exclaimed. He remembered it now, for it reminded him of the bath he'd taken in the water trough—the *Brunnen* as its owner would have called it. *Brunnen, Brunn, Hickelbrunn. That must be how the town got its name.*

The ride into the country was longer than anticipated. When the two couples entered Hickelbrunn, the main street was devoid of people. It was still early in the morning, and life in a small town is quiet in comparison to hustling and bustling city life.

"Let's ask someone," Tony said. The bakery had just opened moments ago, and the smell of freshly baked bread was already filling the parking lot.

They all entered, for the aroma of fresh-baked goods was just too inviting. It was just a moment after they stated their business—namely, finding the road to the castle—that Adelheid had entered the shop.

CHAPTER 22

Adelheid kept herself busy. Even when there were no chores to be carried out, she wandered around her estate to see if she had missed anything. Perhaps some weeds that might have grown back, or a tool in need of repair. Today she stopped to pivot in slow motion, as if to assess the parcel of her remaining land.

Back when Otto was still alive and she was in top shape, she had been known for having unusual strength for a woman of her size. Even now, she could still lift things that would normally have taken two people. Like the garden tiller she once had to lift after Philipp had accidentally tipped it over on top of himself. It is said that in times of great stress, a rush of adrenalin gives the human body the momentary strength to perform tasks that would normally be way beyond its ability.

Adelheid resumed her walk. She reminisced about times of splendor, when she, as a young bride, had come to the Schenkenschloss to spend her life with her new husband.

When Johannes Jr. inherited the lumber mill that had been the source of the family's wealth for generations, Otto inherited the castle estate, which had been in the possession of his family for even longer. As *Schlossherr*, he had sole ownership of the land and the structures on it. Thus, when Otto developed a gambling habit, he had no option other than to sell off his inheritance parcel by parcel to cover his ever-present debts. As he and Adelheid were childless, what little land was left would eventually go to the children of Otto's brother.

And the castle? Well, what exactly makes a castle a castle? By definition it is a structure, fortified with thick walls and often surrounded by a moat. Well, if there ever was one at the Schenkenschloss, there was no evidence of it now. A turret projected from its walls, presumably once a lookout tower, but now nothing more than a reference point for tourists. The castle bore no resemblance to that shown on Adelheid's postcards. The windows were empty frames, their glass broken by the region's frequent storms—unusual atmospheric conditions in the area, it was said.

The castle interior still showed some signs of its once imposing grandeur. There were the remains of a staircase, weather-stained marble slabs leading to the upper *Gemächer*, the apartments of its former inhabitants. A spiral staircase, its iron railings and treads now covered in rust, ended in midair. It had once led to the tower.

Adelheid resumed her walk, not really sure what had drawn her to the old castle. Perhaps just to imagine what it would have been like to live in such a place.

Back then there was no electricity and no indoor plumbing; water had to be brought from a well. The spring at the bottom of the castle's well had ceased to run long ago. Now modern pipes brought water to the property from a nearby reservoir. There was electricity, too, a commodity of which Adelheid made little use. She preferred to spend the evenings by candlelight, with a good book to read or some needlework to do. She still preferred to store her food in the cool cellar beneath the house. No bills to pay to run a freezer or refrigerator.

Adelheid had reached the portico, a gaping cleft where once a door had hung. A big wooden door made of solid oak, Adelheid was sure of it. The painting in Otto's study showed it clearly. The postcards reproduced that same painting. The door must have had a lock made of brass, with a key the size of Adelheid's hands. She had seen such keys in museums, along with other artifacts.

Just as she was about to return to her quarters, she noticed something standing out in the interior. Boulders and smaller stones showed through brush that had grown to nearly the height of the turret. But amongst all of this, stuck between some dense weeds, was a piece of paper. It looked like a wrapper from a candy bar.

"Those tourists!" Adelheid lamented. "They just can't adhere to rules!" The Kein Zutritt sign clearly told them to "keep out." It certainly was visible enough. A few steps and a leap onto a boulder brought Adelheid close enough to reach the wrapper. She could not stand litter, but tourists, especially those with children, occasionally made no effort at all to use the disposals, in spite of the fact that Adelheid had set up large buckets marked "Abfall"—trash, in other words.

She stooped to pick up the wrapper. Just as she crumpled it up to dispose of it later, she noticed some writing. She opened up the paper, pressing it against her hip and smoothing out the wrinkles. Then, with a squint—since she used her eyeglasses only around the house, for reading or needlework—she managed to read its contents: "Take a right when you get to the fork in the road, walk another quarter of a kilometer, and you will see the turret...."

Adelheid didn't finish the sentence. These were instructions to her estate. But so what? Tourists asked for directions to the castle all the time, and perhaps for lack of writing paper, someone had used a candy wrapper instead. Nothing unusual about that. It was the next sentence that got Adelheid's attention: "Look for a marker," it read. What marker?

Adelheid wondered. To the best of her knowledge, there never was a marker on the way to the castle. What really puzzled her, though, was the final statement. "And a pile of stones!" it said.

Not wanting to spend any more time on figuring out where such a marker might be, she returned to her quarters. On the way back, she disposed of her find in one of her trash bins.

CHAPTER 23

"We've got to wait," Tony decided. Resignation echoed in his voice. "It can't be too long, though," he continued. "Going up there during a full moon is just too risky."

"Well, are you sure the stuff is inside the castle?" Ludwig asked.

"No, I'm not!" Tony said impatiently. "But we've got to start somewhere! First we've got to find that marker."

Their first trip to the castle—in the dark of night, with only a flashlight—had been a disaster. Leaving their women behind at the Inn, Tony and Ludwig had climbed the hill where the woods bordered an open field. Vague memories overcame Tony, images from that night fourteen years ago, when he found himself climbing up this very hill with loot in hand and the law in pursuit. He and Ludwig had decided to leave the road and instead approach the property from its back side. It took a little longer, but it was safer this way.

Up close, the castle was not at all what they had expected to find. What little they could see was nothing more than a ruin. "A pile of rubble!" Tony concluded.

Otto had spoken of a marker and a pile of stones. But having been out of touch with him since, well, since Tony had left the jewels in his care, they would have to find the marker on their own.

Their snooping missions had revealed that Otto had passed away years ago. So there would be no reunion with Otto.

They were on their own. All they had was a slip of paper with a diagram of the estate layout, but no information on the marker and the pile of stones.

Flashlights in hand, they climbed through the interior of the ruin. There were weeds all over, including stinging nettle, a plant of the genus *Urtica,* which they discovered as they brushed against the minute stinging hairs. "Verdammt!" Tony heard Ludwig swear in the dark.

Suddenly, a noise aroused their attention. They were not alone. Frozen in their tracks, they waited. There it was again! A faint squeak that undoubtedly came from an animal. Tony relaxed. It was a Fledermaus, a bat, simply out to catch its supper.

Having not really prepared for what they wanted to accomplish, they realized that going any further was useless. They would have to come back by daylight to resume their search for the marker, the pile of stones, and—eureka!—the treasure!

Posing as tourists should make the job a lot easier, Tony thought. This poking around by night... well, Tony couldn't help but compare the two of them to a pair of bumbling criminals.

CHAPTER 24

t was still early when Philipp stopped by to do some pruning down in the orchard. He picked up the necessary tools from the shed, including the canvas bag hanging from its nail in the rafters. In it were pruning shears, a small saw, and a few packages of seeds left over from the previous spring's planting. With a ladder balanced across his shoulder, he was on his way.

"You've got company coming, ma'am!" he alerted Adelheid as he passed by her open kitchen window. Then he doffed his hat to the visitors, acknowledged their greetings, and continued on his way.

"Did you see that?" Tony whispered excitedly.

"Did I see what?" Ludwig replied.

"The bag!" Tony continued. "He had the bag!"

Ludwig, still unsure of what Tony was talking about, replied calmly, "What bag, Tony?"

Impatient, Tony said, "That man who just passed us"—he took a deep breath—"He was carrying our bag!"

Finally Ludwig understood. He had seen the bag before, of course, but how should he remember what it looked like after so many years?

Adelheid emerged from the kitchen. "Guten Morgen!" she said with a smile. Those faces! Where had she seen them before? Oh yes! In the bakery, only a week earlier. And hadn't Margarete expressed concern about Adelheid's well-being after their nosy inquiries?

It's them all right, she concluded as she looked them over. But now her look turned into a stare, fixed on the hands of one of the men as he unwrapped a candy bar and took a bite of it. Noticing Adelheid's startled look, he laughed. "Oh, it's my blood sugar you see! Hypoglycemia!" he explained. "When it's low, I need to eat something sweet."

Adelheid couldn't have cared less about his blood sugar, low or high. It was the paper in which his sweets were wrapped that had caught her attention. Only the day before she had found such a wrapper amongst the sticks and stones of the castle.

If Adelheid had not worried before about Margarete's concerns, she now had to admit that strange things were happening. First the encounter in the bakery, then the wrapper in the castle with its writings about a marker and a pile of stones. The same kind of wrapper the man was now holding in his hands.

This was just too much of a coincidence.

"Would you like to buy some postcards?" Adelheid offered. She tried to remain calm, pretending not to recognize them.

Ludwig obliged by buying two cards, which he grudgingly paid for out of his dwindling funds.

"Danke schön!" Adelheid thanked him, and without further comment, she walked away.

Yes, indeed, they were up to something! Adelheid was sure of that. And it must have something to do with the wrapper she had found in the castle. She continued her walk. She decided to look up Philipp down by the fruit trees. Perhaps he might need some help. He too was getting on in age, and Adelheid was concerned. *What if he slipped and fell off the ladder?*

she pondered. He could lay there with broken bones and not a soul would hear his cries for help.

"Everything going all right?" Adelheid asked as she approached the orchard.

"Just fine!" Philipp assured her. "The apple trees aren't doing so well, though," he reported. "And the plums... well, I think we've got the worm in them again this year."

This was bad news for Adelheid. The fruit was a big part of her stability. She did a lot of canning, and when the harvest was especially kind, she sold the plums to Margarete, whose Zwetschgenkuchen was the best plum cake in the region.

Philipp descended from his post and moved on to the next tree to repeat his task. He cut off the dead branches and piled them neatly on top of each other to be bundled for use as kindling in Adelheid's fireplace.

Adelheid found herself still preoccupied with those strangers, who must still have been looking at the castle, for she had not seen them leave.

"Strange folks, those tourists!" she wondered out loud.

"They must really like to hike up here!" Philipp mentioned casually.

"What do you mean, Philipp?" Adelheid asked, curious.

"Seen them the other night—the two men, that is—climbing up the hill when it was already getting dark! Silly, if you ask me," he concluded, shaking his head.

Adelheid's ears perked. She stepped closer, making sure her voice would not carry too far, should the strangers still be around.

"What do you mean, Philipp? Tell me!" she urged him.

"Well, ma'am, I really didn't want to worry you too much, but I'll be a monkey's uncle if they aren't up to something!"

Adelheid couldn't agree with him more. She too had realized that they were looking for something... but what?

CHAPTER 25

The next morning, as on every weekday morning, Adelheid made her way to Hickelbrunn. The weekend was coming up, and the stores would be busy with shoppers. Today's trip included a stop at the library, where she would return some books and pick up new ones to be read over the weekend.

As her eyes wandered over the titles in one of the sections, she noticed in the corner of her eye a familiar face. It was one of the women again. A pile of dated newspapers lay in front of her, but her eyes read only the headlines before she put each copy aside to read the next one.

That's odd! Adelheid thought. But then she figured that the tourist was looking for some past event that had merited headlines, something unusual, or—*could it have something to do with the wrapper?*

She decided to stay out of sight. She didn't want to be noticed by that woman, who obviously was up to something. Adelheid pretended to read, though it was at the moment the last thing on her mind. As she leafed through book after book, she slowly backed up to disappear behind the next row of shelves. From there she could watch without being seen herself.

Just then, the woman rose from her chair and walked up to the desk, where she briefly talked with the librarian. Then, without further ado, she left the premises.

Adelheid's curiosity peaked again. She approached the woman behind the desk.

"Ah, the countess!" said the librarian. "Find something good?" Adelheid laid down the book she had held in her hands, but she did not answer. Instead, she leaned forward and lowered her voice. "I don't mean to be nosy," she began with a chuckle, "but the woman just now, what exactly was she looking for?"

"Oh!" The librarian smiled, surprised by Adelheid's request, but she obliged with an answer. "Well, she was a historian. She claimed to be looking for information about an event that happened some fourteen years ago."

"What event?" Adelheid interrupted.

"Beats me!" The librarian laughed. "I wasn't even here then, I was in England."

"When did you say this—ahem—'event' was to have happened?" Adelheid pressed.

"Can't tell you more than that!" the woman continued, "just that it happened some fourteen years ago. I told her she had to check through the microfiche to which all the older newspapers have been converted. But the woman decided that she had no time for that."

"So, how old were the papers she checked out?" Adelheid asked, pointing to the stack on the table.

"Oh, those!" the librarian exclaimed. "As a matter of fact, they were just brought in the other day! The Riegler estate, you know. Old Riegler never threw anything away, it seems, so the kids brought a whole bunch of books to donate. The newspapers were just part of it."

"Could I see those micro things?" Adelheid asked, a little hesitance in her request.

"Microfiche?" the woman filled in. "Of course, Countess!" With a wave of her hand, she motioned to Adelheid to follow.

They entered a small room near the end of a long corridor lined with shelf upon shelf of books. There was a desk with a chair and a monitor. Next to the desk was a cabinet filled with small tape discs that were unfamiliar to Adelheid.

Progress! she thought. *What will they think of next?*

A quick look in a logbook gave her the code and number under which the desired microfiche could be found. A short lesson on how to work the monitor followed.

"Good luck!" the woman said and waved at Adelheid as she closed the door behind herself.

Adelheid was excited. What would she find on those discs? What secrets did they hold?

She too was only interested in the headlines, so the task was not as tedious as she had feared at first. One by one she looked at them. A headline appeared that she had not counted on. "Count Otto von Schleppmeister succumbs to heart attack!" the screen yelled out.

A sudden sadness overcame Adelheid. She herself had kept the newspaper of that day. It was still in the drawer where she kept old memorabilia. But this was not the time to dwell on memories. She had to find what that woman had been searching for, whatever it was.

She was just about to give up when another headline graced her screen: "Robbery pursuit leads through Hickelbrunn!" She looked at the date and couldn't believe her eyes. It had happened only three days before Otto—a sudden shudder befell her.

"Dear God!" she gasped. *Could it be that Otto had something to do with this?* she wondered. She read the remains of the story: "Police lost the trail after they found the abandoned getaway car."

She reached for the pen and notepad that lay nearby. Hastily she scribbled down some noteworthy items before returning to the common area.

"Did you find what you were looking for?" the librarian asked as Adelheid passed by her desk.

"Yes, thank you!" she replied without turning around, and with that she disappeared into the street.

"She forgot her book!" the librarian said to herself as she picked it up to return it to its proper slot.

CHAPTER 26

*L*udwig unwrapped another one of his candy bars.

"You shouldn't eat so many sweets!" Soraya lamented.

"It's for medicinal purposes, don't you see?" he explained. Then, sounding more concerned, he added, "I hope I didn't lose my notes up at the castle again, where someone might find them."

"But you already know how to get to the castle, why would you?"

"Yes, of course!" Ludwig interrupted her. "But the notes on the wrapper, if someone finds them, they might bring on suspicion."

He didn't bother to go into any more detail. He was too busy with planning their next move.

"Did Maggie have any luck at the library?" he asked.

"I'm not sure!" Soraya answered as she filed her nails. "What was she looking for, anyway?"

"Oh," Ludwig answered, then paused before he continued. "Just information about... you know, just to find out what the local paper had to say about... you know...."

"The heist?" Soraya finished.

"Shhh!" Ludwig whispered. "Those walls might have ears. You mustn't use words like that!"

Soraya laughed. "Then what would you call it?"

Ludwig never had a chance to answer. A knock on the door announced the arrival of Tony and Maggie, who had come to join them in another one of their planning sessions.

CHAPTER 27

*I*n the meantime, Adelheid had decided to do some baking. It was a cool day, but too early in the season to burn some logs in the fireplace. As she busied herself in the kitchen, there was a knock on the door. One quick glance out the window assured her that it was safe to open the door.

"Philipp!" she said, surprised. "I didn't expect you until...."

"I didn't want to wait until tomorrow!" he interrupted, concern in his voice.

"Come in!" Adelheid offered. "Here, have a seat." She pointed to a chair from which she quickly swept off a pile of laundry she had meant to fold later.

Philipp sat down, hat in hand, and began to talk. "Those folks, you know, those strangers we've been seeing snooping around?" He paused as if waiting for Adelheid to say something. When she didn't, he continued. "Saw them over by the castle, all four of them. And from the looks of it, they were about to do some digging."

"Digging?" Adelheid jumped up from her chair as her voice rose to a volume that startled Philipp. "Where?"

"Can't really tell for sure, ma'am," he said, scratching his head. "First, they were in the castle, then they were *behind* the castle, then...."

"But *where* did they dig, Philipp?" Adelheid asked anxiously.

Philipp got up and walked across the room to where a broom was resting against the wall. "Here," he said, using the upside-down broom to simulate digging. He took a few more steps and then stopped, and *boom, boom, boom,* the broom pounded on the wooden floor. He turned to walk to the far end of the room and repeated his demonstration.

Adelheid sat, her head resting between her hands.

Looking concerned, Philipp asked, "Do you want me to call the police?"

Adelheid shook her head. "Absolutely not!" she exclaimed. And then, more calmly, "I wouldn't want the tourists to get any wrong ideas."

The real reason was a different one. If Otto was involved with them, which by now she was certain was the case, she wouldn't want them to uncover anything that could reveal Otto's shady past.

"No Philipp, no police!" *At least not yet,* she concluded.

82

CHAPTER 28

After Philipp had left, Adelheid remained in her chair, her head still resting in her hands. Minutes passed like hours before she rose to visit Otto's study. She hadn't used this room herself since his death. The memories were too painful.

She still remembered the morning when she checked Otto's bedroom after he failed to show up for breakfast. Shocked to find that he had not slept in his bed, she checked his study and found him there.

Even now she could not rid herself of the thought that what had appeared to be a suicide was perhaps a murder staged to look like a suicide. For one thing, the revolver was still in Otto's hand – his left hand! Otto was right handed. She still wondered if the shot she'd heard back then had really come from Otto's gun or had she just been dreaming... She also remembered hearing voices that morning. But again—were those real or merely something in her dreams? A shudder overcame here. "Dear Lord. Was Otto murdered? What if there was foul play in his demise? Should she have mentioned such suspicions to the authorities? But this was no longer an option, so she had to leave it at that. And for now, she had to do what brought her here in the first place.

A quick glance at the desk drawer confirmed what she had already known. Who would hide anything in a desk? That's the first place one would look—at least, that's what they did in the movies.

The safe! Well that, too, would be too obvious. Besides, she had seen everything in it many times already when, after Otto's passing, she had to attend to his unfinished business affairs. She glanced around the room. The bookshelf! Could there be something hidden amongst the books? She suddenly realized that she didn't even know what she expected to find. If there were jewels, as she surmised, they must be buried somewhere outside—that would explain the tourists' poking around. *The crooks must know about it!*

But they do not know where the jewels are buried, she realized. She suddenly remembered the candy wrapper. Something about a "marker," it had read. *That's it!* she concluded. *They are looking for a marker!*

She decided to resume her search for the marker the next day. But just as she turned to close the door behind her, her eyes fell upon a small dowel sticking out of a tall vase that was otherwise empty. Something told her to check that vase and its contents. When she pulled out the dowel, she found a small ribbon attached to its end. Surely it had nothing to do with her search. She was about to return it to the shelf when she noticed a piece of paper on the bottom of the vase.

Now Adelheid really got excited.

The neck of the vase was too narrow for her hand to fit, but she retrieved it with a nearby letter opener. Before she unfolded it, she sat down in a chair.

"Look for a marker!" the note read. "Then walk ten meters north, where you will find the pile of stones."

There it was again! Directions to find a marker and a pile of stones!

She had to find that pile of stones! She was sure of that. *And then... well, one thing at a time,* she decided, and with that she returned the vase and its contents to their proper place and closed the door behind her.

"The only way we can dig around up there is without the old woman around!" Tony concluded while scratching his head. "Any suggestions?" he added.

Ludwig spoke up, not too sure of exactly what he was trying to say. "Let's, ah, coax her away from up there... by...."

"By sending her to a movie!" Maggie finished.

"Let's get real, Maggie-girl," Tony said, a little annoyed by her unrealistic idea. "The last time that woman saw a movie theater from the inside was probably when you were still in your diapers!"

Now Maggie was annoyed. "Give me some credit, Tony!" she pouted, "I may not be as smart as you, but I've had some good ideas before, like the time when—"

"Yeah, yeah, yeah!" Tony said impatiently. "Let's concentrate on our mission, and—"

"I saw her again at the bakery today!" Soraya interrupted. "That's the third time I have seen her there. Every day she buys some stuff there, every day...." Her voice trailed off as she saw three heads turning in her direction.

"That's it!" Tony explained, pounding his fist on the table. Then, leaning forward, he laid out his plan.

"You, Maggie-girl, and you, Soraya, wait for her arrival at the bakery—out of sight of course." He stopped to think for a minute and then continued. "Then you'll have to find a way to keep her from returning for at least a couple of hours! A couple of hours, that's all we need!"

"How?" Maggie asked innocently.

"How what?" Tony asked back.

"How are we keeping her from returning?" Maggie asked with a blank stare.

"You'll think of something," he said, and before Maggie had a chance to ask any more questions, he turned to Ludwig.

"Okay, first we'll—"

CHAPTER 30

Thieves or no thieves, Adelheid made her way into town for her daily shopping. As she pedaled into the parking lot of the bakery, she noticed two women standing nearby. Paying them little heed, she entered the store, where Margarete was already waiting for her.

"They were here!" she blurted out. "Those women were here!" Adelheid turned around and walked to the store window, from which she could see the two women outside. Now she recognized them. *Where are the men?* she wondered. She had always seen them together before. Then she knew. *Something is going on this very moment, up at the castle!*

"I have to leave!" she called out to Margarete, and with that she was out the door.

"Do you want me to call the pol—?" Margarete asked, but Adelheid was already gone.

All Margarete could see was the two women in the parking lot, who were engaged in a conversation that didn't seem to be of the friendly kind. Their mission had failed.

CHAPTER 31

The two men had again taken the back road to the castle. They brought along a pickaxe they had found in the courtyard of the Inn. So as not to arouse suspicion, they had wrapped it into a blanket taken from one of the Inn's beds.

"Let's go over it again," Tony began. He was breathing heavily as they climbed toward the wooded area through which they had to pass. "I'll find the spot while you stand watch for the old woman." Ludwig just kept on walking behind Tony, nodding as he listened to Tony's plan.

"Are you listening?" Tony huffed, looking back at Ludwig.

"Yes, I hear you," Ludwig grunted, "but I can't talk and climb mountains at the same time." He emphasized "mountain" even though the incline was no more than a hill.

They reached the other side of the wooded land, where it abruptly opened up into a meadow that gradually declined toward Adelheid's land. From there, a smaller stretch of forest angled off toward an orchard. Off in the distance, they could see a figure moving about.

"What the h—!" Tony spouted with a frown as he noticed the figure slowly walking toward the orchard. *Where the heck did he come from?* he wondered as he determined it to be a man.

Ludwig too could see a man slowly making his way toward the tree-lined land. "It's that old fellow from the other day!"

he concluded. "Remember? We saw him in the yard, the one who carried *our bag!*"

Tony remembered, of course, but could not quite figure out where the old man would fit in the picture. He was too old to be a farmhand, yet there he was with some kind of tool resting on his shoulder. A pitchfork, perhaps, but he was too far away to see for sure.

They reached the perimeter of the compound, never leaving their eyes off the figure in the distance. Their voices now turned into whispers, so as not to carry too far on the breeze.

"Let's start in the back of the stable, then work our way toward the castle," said Tony in a hushed voice. And with that, another one of their poking missions began.

CHAPTER 32

*A*delheid hurriedly pedaled toward her domain. Her mind was working faster than her bicycle wheels. The hill was ahead of her. This is where she would dismount and push the bike beside her. But today she had to make the hill on the bike. Time was of essence. Suddenly she felt a slight rumble, and one look confirmed what she had suspected. The bike had a flat tire.

There was no way that she was going to abandon her plan. She had to stop them from finding the jewels.

There was a shallow ditch beside the road. Quickly, she rolled the bike into it and, after removing her wicker basket, proceeded on foot. She would have to come back later to retrieve the bike. Right now, she had other plans. She had a mission!

As she continued up the hill, she began to doubt her intentions. *So what will I do once I am up there? Will I be able to stop them from digging? This could be dangerous,* she realized. *What if they have a weapon?*

She hesitated for a moment. Should she go back into town and summon the authorities? Or should she try to confront the crooks by herself?

Neither plan was a good idea, she surmised. Otto's past would come to light, and that would be impossible for her to overcome. And confronting them? Of course not!

How silly of me! Me against them! But what next? she pondered as she arrived at the stable. Quickly she walked toward the back of the building, taking care to keep out of sight. She heard voices! Hastily she took cover behind a pile of wood and listened.

"Okay, Ludwig, relax. So we didn't find the marker today! But at least we have covered a pretty good area! Next time we just start *inside* the castle, and then..."

Tony's voice trailed off.

"And then what?" Ludwig wanted to know.

"Well, then there must be a reason why we can't find it," Tony concluded.

"And that is?" Ludwig asked again.

"Because the old lady found it before us, stupid!" Tony answered, irritated. He was beginning to have his doubts. He was tired of those planning missions that kept him awake at night. And with Maggie constantly asking, "How long before we are rich?" Tony had lost all patience with Maggie's growing demands. This was not the Maggie he had once known.

His thoughts returned to the present. "If the old lady got our loot, then we've got to find a way to get it from her, by force if necessary!"

"What makes you think she's got the stuff? Ludwig asked. "If she had it, she wouldn't live like a hermit up here in this godforsaken place!"

"Yeah! I think you are right, Ludwig!" Tony conceded. Then he added, with resignation, "We should have never gotten Otto involved in this! We've got *nothing* now. Nothing. Not one damn...." The voices disappeared into the distance.

CHAPTER 33

$\mathcal{A}$ delheid was devastated. How could he! Her Otto, a crook? Tears filled her eyes as she climbed from her hiding place behind the woodpile. *He must have been insane!* Anger replaced her sorrow, and soon her anger was replaced by fear. She *had* to involve the authorities now, when her life might be in danger.

"By force!" she remembered the man saying. Slowly she walked toward the front of the stable, where Philipp was waiting for her on a bench. At the sight of her he jumped up from his seat and walked toward her.

"Are you all right, ma'am?" he asked, his eyes filled with concern. Adelheid was caught off guard. She struggled for an answer. Should she tell Philipp why those men had been snooping around? But how could she do it without letting on about Otto's involvement?

"We've got a problem, Philipp!" she began as she walked toward the bench. "Sit back down!" She took a seat beside him.

"*We've* got a problem," she repeated. She wanted him to be involved with this problem.

"What kind of problem are we having?" he asked. Of course, he knew that it had to do with those men, for he had been waiting for Adelheid's return to report his own observations.

"It's those folks, isn't it, ma'am?" He already knew the answer. "They were here again just a little while ago," he added. "Back by the chickens." He pointed at the coop.

"Did they see you?" Adelheid asked.

"I don't think so." He shook his head. "They were too busy poking around. I still think you should call the police!" he insisted. Then his eyes scanned the yard, and he asked: "Where is your bicycle, ma'am?"

"Oh! That reminds me," Adelheid blurted out. "I've got a flat tire, so I left it by the roadside. Would you be a dear and pick it up for me, Philipp?" And then she added with a smile, "You are so good at fixing broken things!"

"Of course, ma'am!" Philipp assured her, although he began to wonder why she hadn't just pushed it the rest of the way as she usually did, with or without a flat tire. It was just too steep of an incline to ride it. *What an odd thing to do,* he thought, *unless of course it had something to do with the problem she is talking about.*

How far down the road did you leave it, ma'am?" he asked as he headed toward the road.

"About a quarter kilometer!" she hollered after him, not really sure if he heard her.

She got up from the bench to go inside, only to pivot and return to the woodpile, where she had left her wicker basket when she hid behind it.

She never did tell Philipp about what she had overheard. Perhaps that was best for now. She shouldn't have him worrying about her any more than he already was.

Slowly, she unlocked the door to her quarters. One glance convinced her that everything was in order. No open drawers, no tipped-over lamps as one sees in the movies, and of course the lock bore no signs of having been tampered with. Satisfied with her surroundings, she stripped off her sandals and lowered herself onto the couch, where minutes later she was sound asleep.

Noontime had already passed when a knock on the door awakened her. It was Philipp. "I brought your bike, but I'm afraid I can't fix it this time. This inner tube is pretty old," he explained. "Shall I pick up a new one for it?" he offered.

"That's fine," Adelheid assured him, hoping that it wouldn't take too long to replace the tube. Now, more than ever, she needed that bicycle, she was sure of that.

Adelheid's stomach was letting her know that it was time to have lunch. The nap had lasted longer than she had planned—three hours instead of one. But she must have needed that rest. First that wild trip back from town, and thoughts of how it all would end had kept her awake those last few nights. She looked up as if toward heaven. "Otto dear!" she whispered, "If you can hear me up there, you had better help me with this one!"

A silent prayer concluded her thoughts.

CHAPTER 34

A week had passed, and Adelheid was getting nervous. It had been raining for the entire week. The inner tube for the bike was an older model and had to be ordered from the manufacturer. "A week or two," the man at the store had said. But it was just as well. The rain was not letting up, and the country road had become too muddy to ride on. She would have gotten stuck in the mud had she tried. She missed her daily treat from the bakery, and her staples were getting low. But she had enough canned goods tucked away to hold her over for some time. She definitely wouldn't go hungry.

"Speaking of hungry," she said out loud, "I've got to feed those chickens." She stripped off her house slippers and replaced them with a pair of rubber boots. The path to the chicken coop was saturated, and she could move only slowly.

There were footprints in the mud by the coop, and they were not hers. Adelheid's heart pounded at twice its natural speed, or at least so it seemed as she tried to breathe calmly. She hesitated for a moment. Should she turn around and go back to her quarters to keep out of harm's way?

She knew from her eavesdropping that the crooks were prepared to do anything to get their hands on those jewels. The wooden bolt on the coop was still locked, which meant that no one was inside. She began her chores, but she hurried a little.

When the chickens had been fed, she walked around the back of the coop—no small deed, for the stinging nettles were as high as her hips. She had more or less neglected this area, for none of the tourists would ever venture that far. There was no need to keep it groomed.

She was about to turn back when she noticed something showing through the thicket. With the tree branch that she occasionally used as a cane on muddy days like this, she pushed some of the nettles aside to inspect further.

It was a pile of stones. She wondered how they had gotten there. But Philipp was always finding something to do—he must have removed the stones from the garden, so they were not in the way of the tiller, and decided to deposit them out of sight.

She returned to her quarters and went about her other chores. Then, suddenly, she stopped in her tracks. "Look for a pile of stones!" the note had said. That must be them, the pile of stones first mentioned on the wrapper and then again in the note in the vase in Otto's study.

Yes, of course! She smiled to herself. *That's the pile of stones!* She was sure of it. She sat down to plot out her next move.

CHAPTER 35

The rain had finally stopped, and not a day too soon. The weekend was coming and with it a big festival in town. The annual event brought folks from all over the region. There would be music and food and everything else that comes with such festivities.

Adelheid did not care for big crowds, so she decided to do her weekend shopping early. Once the town filled up with people, it would be hard to stay out of their way.

First, she had to check with Philipp about the bike. He lived only a short way from her place. As she walked toward his cottage, she found it unusual that he was not out and about, since he too was an early riser. But there was no sign of him.

She knocked on the door and heard Philipp's voice: "Come in!"

Philipp was resting on his bed, fully clothed except for one foot that had been stripped of its sock and boot.

"What happened, Philipp?" Adelheid asked as she rushed toward him. "Are you all right? No, of course not! How silly of me to even ask," she said apologetically. "What happened?" She looked for a chair to sit on down near his bed.

"Slipped in the mud and hurt my ankle," he explained.

"How long ago?" Adelheid wanted to know.

"Just this morning, but I'll be fine in a day or two," he assured her. "Will you be okay for a while? I mean, without your bike and all?"

"Never mind about me, Philipp!" Adelheid scolded. "I'll walk if I have to, and you just worry about yourself!"

A check of his ankle confirmed that it was sprained; swelling had doubled it in size. There was no way that he would be walking in a day or two as he claimed.

"I'll bring you some lunch later on," she offered. After wetting a towel in cold water to improvise a cold pack, she wrapped Philipp's ankle and, to make him more comfortable, she removed the boot and sock from his other foot.

"There! Now you stay off your feet!" she ordered, "I'll check with you later!" With that, she was gone.

CHAPTER 36

The weekend had arrived, and with it the population from miles around. The festivities were in full swing. The sun had dried up the roads, and Adelheid decided to catch up on some of her outdoor chores. A week of rain had made the weeds grow twice as fast, and of course her vegetable garden was ready for harvest. The raspberry bushes were brimming with berries, and the flowers filled the air with their fragrance.

"What a beautiful day!" Adelheid said to herself. "Business should be great for the town folks!"

The main street had been converted into an open market. Storeowners had put up tables to offer their wares.

Adelheid stopped to make a decision. Should she pick some berries to bake a fruit pie, or harvest some of the green beans? But neither task was to be completed, for a more important mission was at hand. Another visit from some uninvited guests was about to happen, and Adelheid was ready.

CHAPTER 37

"*L*et's go over it one more time!" Tony instructed the three others. Ludwig was all ears, whereas Soraya looked bored and Maggie was pouting. Her feelings had been hurt by Tony's constant questioning of her competence.

"If you think I am so stupid, then why don't you just go by yourself?" Even though, Maggie wouldn't admit it, she too had her doubts about herself. How would she handle a situation that wasn't a sure thing?

"Maggie-girl!" Tony answered with a hint of sarcasm, "you are in it, and you will take part whether you like it or not, you got that?" His voice now hinted at anger.

"Okay, okay, Tony! I was only kidding!" Maggie lied. "I'll be with you all the way."

Maggie was beginning to be a little afraid of Tony. She knew how angry he could get when things didn't go to his liking. She had hoped that age and prison had changed him somewhat, that he had become mellower in his ways. But lately, with things not going the way he had planned, he had quickly slipped back into his old ways.

"We've got to go through with it today!" Tony continued. "We'll go up there, wait in the woods until dark, and then, well, it will have to be tonight!" He knew he had to convince the others. "It must happen tonight," he repeated, "so let's get on our way!"

CHAPTER 38

The beans will have to wait! Adelheid decided as she made her way back to her quarters. Actually she walked rather leisurely, stopping to pick a flower here and there, yet keeping her eyes focused on the edge of the wooded area up the hill, where she had noticed four figures moving about. Only for a moment, but it had been enough to alert her to their presence.

Once she was out of sight, she hurried the rest of the distance to prepare for her next move. With a bundle of white cloth under her arm, she sat by the window, where she could see the entire stretch of the forest. The sun had already dropped into the far horizon, and it was time to act.

Rather than leaving through the door, which she was sure was being watched, she lowered herself through one of the windows. The tall shrub in front of it kept her from being seen.

So far, so good! she thought with a smile, and quickly she disappeared into the ruins of the castle. Through a narrow crack in the stone structure she could peek outside.

It was too dark by now to see if the foursome was still in the woods. *They must be on their way by now,* Adelheid figured. Just then she heard some voices. Quickly she took up her position.

CHAPTER 39

The four figures slowly made their way toward the castle. Adelheid could see a flashlight switching on and off. She could hear what sounded like a shovel being dropped.

"Shhh," a voice cautioned.

Then, one by one, they climbed over the boulder that partially obstructed the entryway to the castle.

"It's more to the left," Ludwig advised in a hushed voice.

"Are you sure?" Tony questioned.

"I swear I saw it right under that window!" Ludwig whispered.

Adelheid found it hard not to laugh out loud. Her plot had worked. Knowing that the crooks would not stop snooping until they found the marker, she had taken it and placed it in a random spot between some stones inside the castle.

But now the marker was gone, back in Adelheid's hands. It was time for her next move. Before the intruders had entered the ruins, Adelheid had taken up her next position.

"Woooo!" The sound came from above. And again, "Wooo-wooo-wooo!" The invaders stopped in their tracks. Only their heads moved, pivoting to better hear where this eerie noise was coming from.

"Holy Mother of Jesus!" Ludwig blurted out, his voice shaky and louder than Tony cared to hear. "*What is your problem?*" he asked in an equally loud voice.

"Wooo! Wooo!" It came from above! Ludwig, working hard to keep his balance on a big stone, could only point. "Ummm," he stuttered while frantically gesturing toward the spiral staircase that ended in midair.

Tony looked up. He could see something, but he wasn't sure what it was.

A flick on the switch of his flashlight brought the two women scuttling toward the exit, screaming, "A ghost! It's a g-ghost up there!"

"It's Otto's ghost, I tell you," Maggie tried to convince the rest.

Tony too had lost his nerve. Goosebumps covered his bare arms. There, on the "stairway to heaven," as he had dubbed it on an earlier visit, stood a ghoulish figure wrapped in a white cloak, its covered arms flapping like a big bird about to take flight. Now the "Wooo" was replaced by a high-pitched giggle.

"Eeeh!" came another wail from above. There was no need for Tony to give any more instructions. They all fled from the site.

The two women ran toward the road, not caring anymore if anyone saw them. Ludwig had lost all sense of direction. Before the action began, he had felt an urgent need to relieve himself. Unfortunately, the shock of having a close encounter with a ghost emptied his bladder involuntarily. Aimlessly he staggered around in the dark. He could see the outlines of a wooden structure: the chicken coop. Slowly he felt his way forward. A dense mass of weeds was in front of him. Ludwig attempted to leap over them, but instead landed, with a crash and a rattling of leaves, in a batch of stinging nettle.

"Sh-t!" came from his lips. "Sh-t, sh-t, sh-t!" he rumbled while raising himself from the ground.

When Ludwig finally arrived back at the Inn, dawn was breaking. Tony and the two women were up waiting for him.

Soraya and Maggie had been the first to reach their quarters. Once they had reached the highway, they hitched a ride into town, pretending to be on their way to the festivities.

Tony had not been so lucky and ended up walking the entire way. And Ludwig's luck had not been much better. He too had to walk back, for trying to hitch a ride while covered with a rash from the nettles, his pants wet from... well, it would have been a bad choice.

"What took you so long?" the other three asked in unison.

"You don't want to know!" he mumbled as he made his way to the bathroom.

"What is that smell?" Maggie wondered.

Tony could not refrain from a loud chuckle. "I think he wet his pants!" he laughed. "He wet his frick'n pants!"

"Shut up!" Soraya yelled at Tony. "There is no need to make fun of him, he is not a coward."

The door to the bathroom opened and Ludwig emerged, wrapped in a bath towel. His arms were covered with nettle stings.

Soraya walked toward him.

"What on earth happened to you, baby?"

"I walked until I came to the chicken coop, from which I would know how to get to the road," he began. "Then I stumbled over a pile of stones, and before I knew what had happened, I was on the ground in a bunch of those d-mn burning ne—"

"Wait a minute!" Tony interrupted him. "Did you say you stumbled over a pile of stones?"

"That's what I said!"

Tony got up to walk toward him. "Ludwig, my man," he began, "if you weren't a guy I would kiss you!" His face lit up in a smile.

Ludwig's face, however, was more like one big fat question mark.

"Don't you see, Ludwig!? Tony explained. "You just stumbled over our fortune!"

Ludwig was still baffled.

"Don't you remember, the note? 'Look for a pile of stones.'"

Ludwig's face lit up. "You think that's it? The stones I fell over?"

"They have to be!" Tony said with certainty.

"They just... over the years they just got covered up by those weeds."

Now everyone was convinced that Ludwig had found the spot beneath which their fortune was waiting.

But did they dare to go back? Back, where Otto's ghost might be waiting for them?

"Count me out!" Ludwig protested. "There is no way in Hades that I will go back up there again! No way in hell!"

Tony did some arithmetic. "Let's see now," he began, "there are four of us. How many million did they say the loot was worth?"

"Seven and a half or eight," Maggie said. "I can't remember exactly what the papers said."

"Well, let's say eight million," Tony continued. "That's two million per head! Think about it!"

Tony had divided the amount by four, but in reality he had other plans. Why should they, who hadn't spent a day behind bars, reap the same amount as he?

No, Tony thought, *I deserve half, and they—No, I'll take seventy-five percent, and what did the women do to deserve any at all?*

"We'll go back tonight again. On second thought, we'll—"

"I don't know, Tony," Ludwig interrupted. "Frankly, I'm not sure any more if I want—"

"Two million. Ludwig!" Tony reminded him. "Two million, think about it!"

"Okay Tony, you win!" Ludwig said, resigned. "But this will be the absolute last time that I'll set foot in that... that..." He groped for words. "In that ghost-infested pile of rubble!"

"Ludwig! It *will* be the last time!" Tony promised him.

CHAPTER 40

$\mathcal{A}$delheid had watched their departure—or was it their escape?—with great pleasure. Her plot had worked. *It's amazing what a white bedsheet can do,* she laughed to herself. *So they thought I was Otto's ghost!* She wondered if it was Otto's spirit that had given her the idea of playing a ghost to scare them off. *I'll never know,* she concluded as she descended from the "heavenly" staircase.

She heard one of the men stumble and fall, and she emitted another one of her "Wooos" for good measure.

The next morning Adelheid returned to the scene of her performance. The marker, which she had moved the night before, had fallen from her hands while she flapped her "wings." It took no time to find it. She looked around to see if they left anything behind, and sure enough, they had. A shovel lay between another pile of stones overgrown with weeds. Adelheid was about to pick it up when she had another thought.

No, I'll leave it. Let them think I never was aware of their ghostly encounter. She climbed out of the rubble, but instead of returning to her quarters, she walked toward the chicken coop, where some hungry chickens were waiting for their breakfast.

She approached the coop from behind, rather than from the path she usually took when she came from the house. She noticed the spot where one of the men had stumbled the night before. It was the same pile of stones she had discovered

115

earlier. The pile of stones which had to be the pile of stones mentioned in Otto's notes!

Should she dig to find the treasure and turn it over to the authorities? No, that was not an option, for they would wonder how she knew of the jewels' existence and whereabouts.

Suddenly she realized that the crooks, too, must have concluded that this was Otto's pile of stones. The man she saw stumble must have mentioned it. In any case, she was prepared for their return. One more encounter with a ghost would certainly send them scurrying. But no, that wasn't the solution. On the contrary, she *wanted* them to dig up the jewels, to catch them in the act of retrieving stolen goods. But it would take some precise planning on her part if they were to be apprehended before they left town.

She knew they were staying at the local inn. She could warn the innkeeper and have him call the police, once he saw them return. But that again would reveal the fact that she knew about the jewels.

I'll think of something, she decided. Besides, it was early in the morning, and their return, she wagered, would most likely not take place until darkness set in.

Adelheid was wrong.

CHAPTER 41

"This will be a piece of cake!" Tony informed the others. "We'll go in the middle of the day, when the whole town is swinging. Heck, the old lady might even be down there herself," Tony figured, "and if she is up there, let's just do what we have to do, and—"

"And what?" Ludwig asked, fearing that he might already know the answer.

"You just let me worry about that," Tony answered with a wave of his hand.

They had packed their belongings and were ready to depart as soon as they returned from their final attempt to dig up the jewels.

"All set?" Tony asked. "Let's go!"

Even though they didn't care any more about being seen by Adelheid, they decided to hike up through the back woods rather than the open road.

And Adelheid did see them. What she couldn't figure out was, why hadn't they tried to hide from her? Unless— Adelheid's heart began to pound.

Unless they are after me, she concluded. *Now what?* she pondered. That was not what she had anticipated, nor calculated for.

She ran to Otto's study, where a hunting rifle was stored in a cabinet. Quickly she removed it from its casing, only to discover that there was no ammunition. *Well, they won't know that!* she decided, and with that she was on her way to the chicken coop, where a small window framed their arrival.

Adelheid had to act quickly. She was scared, which did not happen too often. Her feisty demeanor in times of peril had kept many would-be intruders at a distance.

"Okay, Otto dear!" she said as she looked skyward, "it's your turn now. You take over!" But she knew she was on her own. Another prayer was in place right now, she thought.

The crooks had taken up their position, just as she expected, by the pile of stones. With a wooden stick they pushed back the nettles to expose the stones beneath. They had retrieved the shovel from the castle. The sound of digging and of stones being moved proved that their mission was in full swing. Not much was said, but when they did speak, Adelheid could hear every word of their conversation.

"Yeah! I think she is down there, swingin' with the rest of them," Tony huffed while catching his breath. Then he said, "There, you take over!" and handed the shovel to Ludwig.

The two women were on the lookout nearby.

"There is no sign of her by the house!" Maggie reported.

"It's like I said," Tony repeated, "she is down there sw—"He stopped in mid-sentence, his eyes and mouth wide open as he raised both arms.

The others, whose backs had been turned, now followed his stare... and found themselves staring into the barrel of a shotgun.

"Move!" said Adelheid. And again: "Move, all of you!" She deepened her voice to express more authority. "Into the coop!" she ordered as her voice became louder.

Perhaps Philipp will hear me! she hoped. But that thought disappeared when she remembered that he was still laid up with a sprained ankle.

One by one they entered the chicken coop. Adelheid slammed the door behind them, turned the wooden bolt, and just for good measure, braced their shovel against the door. A couple of stones from the pile nearby held the shovel in place.

There is no escape possible from this place, Adelheid reassured herself. The window was too small to climb out, and the chicken door was also small enough to prevent any escape.

"There!" she exclaimed. "Take that, scum!" She laughed, and to agitate them even more, she let loose a few of her wooo-woos.

"Now they will know who that ghost was," she giggled as she opened the door to her quarters.

But soon she became serious again. She had to notify the authorities—turn the thieves over for trespassing and... *Well, they'll find out soon enough why those four were trespassing,* she decided.

This would be a good time to have a telephone again, she concluded, but her lifestyle just did not merit such an extra expense. *So, what next?* she pondered. Her bicycle was still in need of repair. Then she remembered what Philipp had said: "It's just like a bicycle, only faster!"

Yes, Philipp's motorcycle! She would have to use it to get into town. *How do you start this thing?* she wondered when she reached the garage where Philipp kept it. She had watched him kick a pedal whenever he took her on errands. She found a small lever on one side. With a swift motion, she swung herself into the seat as if mounting a horse. "A horse, a horse, my kingdom for a horse," she said. "Now who again was that, who said that?"

Yes, a horse would indeed come in handy right now. She had grown up around horses and was an accomplished equestrian in her day. "Well, the motorcycle will have to do!" It took a few kicks before the motor gave a howl. She knew she could control the speed by manipulating the grip on the handlebar. Now all she had to do was get it into gear.

Off in the distance, she could hear her prisoners fighting amongst themselves.

"It's all your fault!" a woman's voice was screaming, "all because you're such a money-hungry jerk!"

"Aren't you all?" Adelheid said as she brought the motorbike into motion. And off she was on her way.

CHAPTER 42

There was a crowd in the distance where the town square opened up to the main road. People were walking along the highway, and cars passed at a snail's pace, waiting to reach the parking area on the opposite side of the square. A group of bikers had assembled nearby. Adelheid decided to join them as she coasted to a halt. There were dozens of them, all dressed in typical biker gear: black leather vests covering their bare torsos, bandanas covering heads, and arms displaying weird tattoos of skulls and heads of animals—one of them even had a small heart inscribed with "Mutter."

Adelheid ended right in their midst. The ride into town had been fairly smooth, except that the wind had caused her braided bun to come apart, leaving her loose hair tangling in part over her face.

"Where is your broom?" one of the bikers chuckled as he looked her up and down.

Adelheid ignored his remark. "I need your help! You must come with me, for there are criminals on my property, jewel robbers! We must turn them over to the police before they can escape!" she blurted out.

"Where are they now, those jewel robbers?" one of them asked.

"In the chicken coop! I locked them in the chicken coop," Adelheid informed him.

"Why don't you ask the police?" He pointed toward the intersection where not one, but two uniformed men were directing traffic.

"But they are busy, can't you see?" she pleaded. The bikers around them nodded in agreement.

"Where are we going?" the big man asked, clearly convinced that this woman was not kidding. This little woman who looked more like a grandmother than a biker chick.

Adelheid quickly gave him the rundown on how she got involved in this mess. "Follow me!" she wanted to say, but she suddenly had a change of heart.

"I'm not sure I should lead you up there, for you see…" She hesitated. "This is the first time I ever drove a motorcycle, and I really don't know how to shift it in high gear and all."

The biker shook his head "You are some gutsy lady, ma'am!" Respect rose in his voice.

"Which one of you is riding solo?" he hollered into the crowd. A couple of bikers raised their hands.

"One of you take… What's your name, ma'am?" he asked.

Adelheid never had a chance to answer. "Guten Tag, Countess!" came a voice from a group of people passing their assembly.

The bikers' heads all turned toward Adelheid, who had mounted the back seat of one of the motorcycles. The back of the bike's driver read "Willie."

"You are the countess from the old castle up there?" the man asked, pointing toward the castle in the distance.

"In the flesh!" Adelheid answered, a little embarrassed as she remembered her messy hair and her otherwise grubby attire.

"Lead the way!" he instructed her. He turned to address the rest of the bikers. "Something about some jewel thieves," he informed them, though the exact nature of their mission was still a little vague to him.

"Take a right," Adelheid shouted over the roar of the motors after they reached the fork in the road. Willie was one of the leaders, and whose torso served as her handhold, just as she had done so many times with Philipp. Only this man's circumference was nearly double that of Philipp's, thanks to an impressive beer belly.

"See the tower up there?" Adelheid pointed from behind. "That's where we are going."

Willie signaled for the rest of the bikers to follow.

Adelheid's—or, rather, Philipp's—bike was left behind with some biker chicks watching over it, for none of the male bikers wanted to be seen riding a *Klapperkasten*—a clattering clunker. No real biker would be caught dead on such a monstrosity.

They had reached the dirt road and shifted gears on the slow incline.

CHAPTER 43

*T*ony was furious! As the sun rose, the chicken coop became hotter and hotter. The chickens themselves had flown the coop and were cackling outside. The stench inside became more and more unbearable as the temperature rose.

Soraya had surrendered to uncontrollable sobbing, while Maggie just stood and stared out the tiny window. Ludwig, the poor soul, had searched for a place to sit. The plank that led to the chicken door had looked suitable enough for a makeshift bench. Unfortunately, that poop-drenched piece of wood was not meant to hold anything more than a few chickens and thus—

Crash! Boom! The wooden board plunged into the poop-drenched straw beneath it. There was dead silence for a moment. But then, all hell broke loose.

"I'll get you for this, Tony!" Ludwig screamed as he emerged from his bath. "I swear, I'll get you for this, you... you bastard!"

The sound of a motorcycle interrupted his furor. The sound became louder. It was a roar now.

"There are bikers coming!" Maggie announced. "One, two... seven!" she yelled out as she pressed her face against the small window.

The bikes came to a stop. Willie had by now heard more of the details. He knew that there was no working phone on the premises, so he had to think of other ways to summon the police.

"One of you ride over to Hetzfeld to get the law," he suggested. "The local cops are too busy today!"

One of the bikers came forward. "I'm a police officer," he stated as he opened his billfold to show his badge. It was his day off, and he had come from another nearby town for the festivities in Hickelbrunn.

"I know the locals are busy directing traffic, but I could summon my people," he offered as he reached for a walkie-talkie in his shirt pocket.

"How long before they would get here?" Willie asked.

"Oh! With their sirens, I'd guess twelve to fifteen minutes," he answered.

"Go for it!" Willie said with a laugh.

After giving directions to the castle over the radio, the man added, "Oh! Be sure to bring enough handcuffs and a couple of cars: there are four of them! Over and out!"

Adelheid let off a big long sigh: "A - m - e - n to that!" She grinned.

BOOK TWO
*T*HE CRUISE

CHAPTER 1

"Oh, how wonderful," Margarete, the woman from the local bakery, exclaimed as she heard of Adelheid's plans of going on a cruise. "You have certainly earned it," she assured the countess.

Margarete was referring, of course, to the reward the countess received from the insurance company for turning in the thieves and returning the jewels to the museum. "And just think—it all started right here," the countess mused, glancing around the shop. She sighed, thinking about her departure the next day on the luxury liner, Fortuna, with its passenger manifest of rich and famous people—and some not so rich and famous, like Adelheid. "I will miss your apple strudel, though." she smiled. "You think they have apple strudel on a ship?"

"How long will you be gone?" Margarete wanted to know. "Just a couple of weeks, Margarete. Can't stay away from your shop for too long," she joked as she left the store. "Have a pleasant trip, Countess," the baker-woman hollered as Adelheid closed the door behind her. "I'm really looking forward to it," Adelheid said mostly to herself as she packed away her treat. With a swift move she mounted her bicycle to return to her quarters.

CHAPTER 2

$\mathcal{P}$hillip, once in Adelheid's employ as the custodian of her estate, and occasional "chauffeur" to Adelheid whenever she needed to go a distance too far for a ride on a bicycle, was now sitting in Adelheid's kitchen, a mug of coffee before him. "I'm really sorry, Countess, that I can't be the one to take you to the train station," he apologized, "It's just… "

"Why Phillip," Adelheid interrupted him laughingly, "I never expected you to take me there. It's just too far to drive on your—your motorcycle," she finally finished her sentence. She wanted to say, "On your old heap of metal that once was a motorcycle." Sure, it still ran, but old as it was it had its moods. But more often than not, it just sat there. "Franzl is taking me," she informed him.

Franz Lohmeier, a farmer who had been renting some of Adelheid's parcels of land, had offered to take her by car. He had some business to take care of in Riem, a city about a two-hour drive from Hickelbrunn.

Adelheid was all set for her journey. Her cloth-covered suitcase, which from the looks of it had seen better days, was sitting by the door, its identification tag dangling from its ribbon fastened to the handle. After one last look to assure herself that all the important information was given, Adelheid nodded to herself. She was satisfied. "Frau Adelheid Schleppmeister" it read. Below her name: "Hickelbrunn, Austria."

There was a reason why Adelheid was not including her inherited title. She was first of all too modest to flaunt her ancestry. And secondly, she was tired of people who liked to attach themselves to the aristocracy for no other reason than to be seen in the company of such folks. So as far as her fellow travelers were concerned, once she boarded the Fortuna she was nothing more than a "little old lady" from some town, somewhere in Austria.

CHAPTER 3

"Welcome aboard, Madam," a young man in a white-as-snow uniform with gold buttons and a nametag pinned to his breast pocket greeted her. "Frau Schleppmeister?" he asked to make sure he had the right person in front of him as he glanced at the clipboard in his hands.

"That would be me," Adelheid confirmed.

I've got to get used to this "Frau" thing, she thought. That self-imposed status was something Adelheid decided to have some fun with. "Let them think I am some poor old woman who probably won a cruise by entering some kind of contest or whatever." Well, if people were to judge her by her attire, it could very well be the case. Fashion never was one of Adelheid's concerns. She had comfort in mind. Comfortable shoes as well as clothes were what she preferred.

"I'll take you to your cabin," the man in the white uniform informed her. "My name is Salvador," he introduced himself. A slight accent reflected his native tongue, Italian. And why not? The cruise line was owned by an Italian concern. The Fortuna was not their only passenger ship. They also owned smaller vessels, which were used for day-cruises and sight-seeing excursions which usually left by dawn and returned by the end of the day.

The Fortuna was a luxury liner capable of holding a thousand passengers and a crew of two hundred, or so the brochure read. There was page after page of information, including a diagram and layout of *what* is *where* and so forth. But Adelheid was too tired to read on. With a big yawn she laid the brochure back on the nightstand where she had found it. The train ride and then the boarding procedures were just a little too much. She was exhausted. She was even too tired to take in the dinner, tempting as it sounded. "Braised lamb chops with linguine pasta," the menu read.

"Well, my sandwich will hold me over till breakfast," she decided. The sandwich made from Margarete's hearty rye bread, topped with smoked ham, was still in Adelheid's travel pouch. She never did get a chance to eat any of it, for the train had a dining car with inviting delicacies on the menu, including Applestrudel, which, Adelheid found out, could not match Margarete's mouthwatering creations.

There was a knock on the door of her cabin. Adelheid rose from the edge of her bed where she was about to disrobe to open the door. A young woman smiled at her. "What time would you like to be awakened, Madam?"

"Oh, no need for that," Adelheid assured her. "I'll be awake before the sun comes up."

The young woman's smile turned into a somewhat puzzled look. "Have a pleasant goodnight, Madam," she offered, and away she turned to knock on the door across from Adelheid's.

Wearily, Adelheid opened her luggage to remove a nightgown. "The rest can wait till morning," she yawned. And with that she slid under the down covers of her bed.

CHAPTER 4

*A*delheid, tired as she was, did not have a restful night. Sleeping in a strange bed, for one. And second, there was noise, albeit never more than a rumble. Given that this was a luxury liner, it seemed odd. Was this normal? Was she to endure this every night?

There was activity outside her cabin door. She glanced at her wristwatch. It was a quarter past seven a.m. "Wow," Adelheid chuckled. "And I was the one bragging about being up before sunrise."Well, at least she wouldn't miss breakfast, which was served from six to nine. After a quick shower and unpacking the rest of her luggage, she readied herself to seek out the dining room.

"Excuse me," Adelheid approached a man as he passed her in the corridor. "Where can I find the dining room?"

"Which one?" the man wanted to know.

Adelheid, a little startled, replied, "The one where I can have some breakfast?"

"They all serve breakfast, Madam," he laughed.

"Of course," Adelheid smiled, a little embarrassed. How could she forget. It was all explained in that glossy booklet she had received from the travel agency. She had leafed through it at the time, but never really read it from cover to cover. It was still where she had left it on the kitchen table back home.

"Take a right after you get off the elevator," the young man instructed her. "You can't miss it," he assured her as he disappeared into one of the cabins along the corridor.

Adelheid followed his instructions and soon found herself in a large room, which could best be described as an Italian-style bistro. There were checkered tablecloths covering small round tables positioned around the perimeter of the room. And windows everywhere so no matter where you sat, you could see outside. There was a deck on one side and a swimming pool on the other, with a strange looking structure here and there.

Probably some sort of exercise equipment, Adelheid concluded. Adelheid, out of touch with the world beyond her beloved estate since her Otto died, had never kept up with the progress going on in the rest of the world. Sure, she read the newspapers, listened to her radio, and collected bits and pieces of information just chatting with friends like Margarete the baker-woman or Phillip and Franz Lohmeier.

But now she found herself in a world she had to catch up with. "But so what?" she concluded as she filled her plate with some inviting morsels spread out before her on a buffet that took in the entire width of the room. There were omelets, "frittatas" as they were called in Italian. Soft-boiled eggs were lined up in small egg cuplets, and Adelheid's favorite, eggs benedict, was just being added by one of the chefs.

"I've got to have one of those," Adelheid smiled at the chef. With some fresh fruit and a good cup of coffee, Adelheid was in heaven.

CHAPTER 5

"May I join you?" an elderly gentleman asked Adelheid as he stood before her holding a tray filled with pastry.

"Why, of course, please do," Adelheid quickly replied, shifting her plate to make space on the little table now holding her empty dishes. A small vase with fresh flowers in the center of the table was pushed off to the side. "There," she said with a smile. "Let me help you with your tray," she offered when she noticed him struggling to unload its contents onto the table.

There was a cane hanging from his arm, which made balancing the tray somewhat difficult. Quickly, Adelheid rose from her chair to help. The unoccupied table next to hers was already holding Adelheid's empty tray, so she placed the man's empty tray from his slightly trembling hands there.

"Thank you so much, you are very kind," the man complied, seating himself across from her. But quickly he rose again to introduce himself with a slight bow. "My name is Viktor, Viktor Eichelberger."

Adelheid reached across to shake his outstretched hand. "Very nice to meet you," she smiled. "I'm Adelheid von—I'm Adelheid Schleppmeister," she corrected herself.

Adelheid noticed a familiar dialect in his speech and asked, "Are you Austrian?"

"Indeed I am," he proclaimed proudly. "Born and raised in Vienna."

"So am I!" Adelheid exclaimed. "I mean, I'm Austrian, too," she laughed. "But I have been in Vienna in my youth. School and all, you know," she explained.

"Well, now I am *really* glad I chose your table," Viktor laughed. "I hope you don't mind if I join you from here on, I mean, to sit with you when I take my meals," he asked with some hesitation.

"On the contrary!" Adelheid exclaimed. "I was just going to ask you the same question."

"Well now," Viktor declared, "I guess that makes us travel partners or—or—"

"Friends," Adelheid finished his sentence.

"Friends indeed!" Viktor agreed. "Friends indeed"

CHAPTER 6

$\mathcal{A}$ delheid was still a little tired, so after departing from the Bistro she decided to return to her cabin, hoping to catch up on a few more hours of sleep. But mid-way to her quarters she turned around. The elevator to one of the upper decks was nearby.

"Better yet, I find myself one of those deck chairs or chaise lounges to take my nap," she decided. The sky was without a cloud and the sun was halfway up the horizon. It was mid-morning. Adelheid quickly dozed off, and by the time she awoke, the sun was already high above in the sky.

A quick glance at her watch confirmed that it was almost noon. *Lunchtime already?* she thought. She was still full from that rich breakfast. *Should I eat again? Well, a promise is a promise,* she decided. She had told Viktor that she would meet with him for lunch. "You decide which dining room we should visit," she had suggested.

"Let's just meet starboard by elevator number five, and I will take you to the Commodore's Lounge," he had suggested. "It's a lovely place, I dined there last night."

Adelheid had a little trouble rising from the chaise lounge in which she had chosen to take her nap.

"I see you could use a little help," a young voice came from behind. "Let me help you." A woman who appeared in her thirties approached Adelheid. "Grazie, molti grazie," Adelheid thanked her, hoping that her reply was in the language of the woman's nationality.

Her jet-black hair and deep brown eyes gave her away. The woman was indeed Italian—a fellow passenger like Adelheid. A tennis racket in her hands confirmed Adelheid's assumption. "My name is Lidia." The young woman now spoke in German, with just a trace of accent in her speech.

"Vielen Dauk für Ihre Hilfe, Lidia," Adelheid thanked her, but decided not to give out her own name, at least for the time being.

The encounter with Lidia was not to be the last one, as Adelheid soon found out. Lidia seemed to pop up out of nowhere, no matter what section of the ship Adelheid found herself in.

Was it coincidence? Perhaps. Or, was it well-planned encounters? Adelheid decided that it was just coincidence. As far as she was concerned, there wasn't a soul on this ship— aside Viktor and a few crewmembers—who knew who she was. She was Frau Schleppmeister, the "little old lady" from some small town somewhere in Austria.

CHAPTER 7

*L*idia Frattera was not a happy woman. This cruise—at least up to now—was not what she had expected.

"Don't do anything until the others come aboard. And—be careful," José Batali had warned her as he dropped her off in front of the terminal, where passengers pass through before boarding a vessel.

"I'll do my best," she had promised, and disappeared with a wave. Her luggage was minimal. A carry-on with wheels attached and straps that served as support when converted into a backpack. Its contents were what one usually carries when going on a cruise. There were pieces of clothing, including a bathing suit, a toothbrush and sun tan lotion. There were also a few items that most women won't do without, like makeup. But that was it. Or was it?

After unpacking her clothes, she neatly hung them on the hangers that were tangled on a rod behind one of the mirrored sliding doors of a wardrobe. A couple of built-in drawers with a shelf above them was the rest of the cabin's interior. There was a gun wrapped in one of her sweaters. Carefully, she removed it to stow it away.

But where? It must not be found by anyone. The cleaning crew that serviced the passenger cabins might find it, and the consequences could be—

"Well, let's not even think about it," she abandoned her fears. "I'm here on a mission, a job, for which I volunteered.

But chances were that I would have been assigned to it anyway," she concluded. This could very well have been the case, since she, Lidia, was the only one in her group who'd mastered four languages. Well, three and a half. Her German was about as flawless as her native Italian, since her mother was of German stock. Her English was acquired in school, and her French—well, it consisted mostly of a vocabulary that lovers would use among themselves.

There were a couple more items that she had retrieved from her carry-on. A camera—actually, it was an evening purse or a clutch bag, with a camera cleverly built into its flap. The other was a tape recorder in the shape of a pen. A listening device, one of the world's newest inventions—well, actually not that new. These gadgets have been around for a while, but they were new in Lidia's life. Only once did she have to use one, but that was another story.

Lidia slowly scanned the room. "Where can I hide these?" she pondered. Without success in finding a proper place to stow away her "tools," as she called them, she placed them—at least for the time being—in one of the wardrobe drawers.

She looked at her wristwatch. Only an hour had passed since she boarded. The ship would not depart for another three hours. Should she go deck-side and watch the hustle and bustle, the crewmembers scurrying, escorting new arrivals to their assigned cabins?

"No," she decided. And with that she slipped off her shoes and flopped down on her bed to relax for a while. There was a booklet on the nightstand. Lazily, she reached to pick it up. A loose piece of paper fell from it and slid under the nearby stuffed chair. Lidia wasn't about to rise up to retrieve it. "It will still be there later," she surmised.

The booklet held the usual information that every passenger should know. Rules and regulations, the amenities offered and, of course, the time during which meals were served. There was also a round-the-clock service for those traveling first class. But Lidia was in tourist class and her accommodations, albeit quite comfortable and functional, were not nearly as luxurious as those one deck above hers.

She was about to return the booklet to its place on the nightstand when a picture caught her eye. It was a posed photo. A pretty model holding a piece of jewelry which she was about to place into a built-in safe.

"Of course!" Lidia jumped up from her bed.

"Every stateroom is equipped with a small safe for your personal valuables," it read beneath the photo. "But where is it?" Lidia wondered. She had already searched the room in hopes of finding a safe place to hide her tools. But there was nothing that resembled a safe. "Every stateroom," she mumbled to herself. Perhaps it's just the first class section where they have them. Besides, Lidia's room was not exactly what would qualify as a "stateroom." A cabin, yes. But not a stateroom. Resigned, she returned to her bed, and with nothing else to do, she decided to take a nap.

CHAPTER 8

tarboard. What is that again? Adelheid tried to remember. *Was it the left side, or, the right side of the ship?* she pondered.

"Meet me at the starboard by elevator number five," she remembered Viktor's words.

"Excuse me," Adelheid asked a passing couple, "could you tell me which way is elevator number five?"

"Do you want number five starboard or portside?" the couple wanted to know.

"Starboard," Adelheid quickly replied.

"It's opposite from where we are now," the couple advised her.

"Thank you kindly." Adelheid waved as she made her way to the opposite side of the vessel. A glance toward the water told her that she was facing forward. Was it "head" as opposed to "aft"? Well, she was on the left side, or whatever it was called in ship lingo. So the right side of the ship is what's called "starboard." "Try to remember that old girl" she said to herself, as she made her way toward elevator number five—*starboard.*

Viktor was already waiting, sitting nearby on a bench, his hands resting on the grip of his cane.

"Sorry if I'm late," Adelheid excused herself. "I've had a little trouble trying to find the starboard side of the ship," she laughed.

"I hope you are hungry" Viktor greeted her. "There is a feast waiting for us."

"Oh my," Adelheid hesitated. "I'm not sure if I can eat so soon again, but I'll certainly try," she laughed as they entered the Commodore Lounge.

The room was already filled with hungry passengers, and the line in front of the buffet table suggested that it could be a while before it would be Adelheid and Viktor's turn to fill their plates.

"Let's go to the bar until the line is gone," Viktor suggested.

"But—but I don't drink," Adelheid confessed with a smile.

"You mean you don't drink alcohol," Viktor corrected her. "Everybody has to drink—to stay alive," he added. "They offer all sorts of drinks," Viktor assured her. "Just tell the bartender what you would like and he will fix it for you."

"Thank you, Herr Eichelberger," Adelheid smiled. "I'll—"

"And another thing," Viktor interrupted her, "my name is Viktor to you, so let's drop the formalities, ok?"

"And you may call me Adelheid," she agreed.

"Nice to meet you—again, Adelheid," Viktor joked as he reached out to shake her hand.

"Likewise, I'm sure," Adelheid chuckled.

"I hope you don't take this the wrong way," Adelheid hesitated as she took one last sip from her tall glass of iced tea, "but would you like to join me in my cabin for a game of chess?"

Viktor's eyes widened. "How did you know I play chess?" he asked, surprised.

"I didn't, " Adelheid laughed. "I just had a hunch that you might know the game," she lied.

Earlier that day at the breakfast table, during the course of their conversation, Viktor had spoken of an event where a chess game had taken place. He used a term only known to those who know the game.

"I'll be delighted to join you in a game of chess," Viktor answered enthusiastically. "And as far as taking this invitation the wrong way—" Viktor smiled, "would it help if ... I told you that I am a member of the clergy?"

Adelheid looked surprised. "You are a pastor?" she asked.

"Father Viktor at your service," he declared, while again holding out his hand to shake Adelheid's.

"A priest!" Adelheid exclaimed. "A Catholic priest!"

"A retired Catholic priest," Viktor explained. "The cruise was a farewell present from my parishioners"

"What a wonderful gift," Adelheid added. "Then, my cruise was—more or less also a present," she began. "But it's a long story. I'll tell you about it sometime," she promised.

The Commodore Lounge had cleared considerably. Only a few guests stood around the buffet table, perhaps for a refill or some of the dozens of desserts. Viktor was not too hungry, either, so their stay was a short one. Adelheid had chosen a salad and some Italian bread topped with mortadella sausage and slices of avocado.

"What time should I be at your cabin?" Viktor asked.

"Well," Adelheid thought for a minute, "do you usually take a nap in the afternoon? I mean, I don't want to deprive you of any sleep or—"

"I do back home, yes," Viktor confessed. "But this is a pleasure trip, one that might be the last one in my lifetime. So, I want to enjoy every waking moment of it—especially in the company of a charming woman such as you, Adelheid"

"Well, then why not come with me right now?" Adelheid suggested. "Let's stop by the game room and sign out a chessboard."

CHAPTER 10

$\mathcal{A}$delheid's cabin, or stateroom, as the crew called it, was not too far from Viktor's. About five doors down, but on the opposite side of the corridor.

Adelheid had to check her key to assure herself that its number matched the number and letter on the cabin door in front of her.

Cabin 22A it read.

Viktor's cabin was 17 B.

Once settled into their chairs around a small portable table, Adelheid set up the chessboard.

"So-o-o...," Viktor began slowly "... what is the story behind *your* present, I mean, you taking this cruise? Was it your birthday?"

"Oh no," Adelheid smiled, "it was a reward"

"A reward?" Viktor looked puzzled.

"Why don't I tell you all about it," Adelheid offered. "But first, let's get more comfortable," she suggested as she pointed toward a couple of stuffed chairs.

Adelheid was about to begin with her story, about how she locked a bunch of crooks into the chicken coop until the authorities could lead them away—when she stopped in mid-sentence as Viktor raised his hand to motion her to silence. "Before I forget, Adelheid, I want to listen to this noise, this rumble you heard during the night. Perhaps a complaint is in order," he suggested.

Quietly they sat and listened. There was no rumble, not a sound anywhere in the room or outside.

"This is strange," Adelheid wondered. "Why wouldn't it make a noise now, if the source came from the ship's mechanics, the engine or whatever?"

Viktor had a thought. "I shall listen for a noise in *my* cabin tonight. Perhaps I can identify the noise and thus its source. But for now, tell me more about your reward and the story behind it."

"You are some gutsy lady!" Viktor laughed after hearing about Adelheid's encounter with the jewel thieves. "I remember the story well, back then," he continued. "Why, the newspapers were full of details about the heist. The 'Richtenberg Jewels' was it not?" he asked.

Adelheid almost regretted that she had told him. What if he asks how the jewels ended up on her property? Suddenly, as if to retrieve a piece of memory, he put one hand on his forehead while pointing at Adelheid with the other. "You are the countess! Of course, the Countess von Schleppmeister. The one who—well, I'll be—"

"In the flesh," Adelheid confessed. And then added as an afterthought, "But let this be *our* secret, Viktor."

"Why, of course, Frau Schleppmeister," he promised, with the emphasis on *Frau*. "Oh, and will you promise not to let on that I am a priest?"

"Yes!" Adelheid laughed, "But that's almost impossible, since all the crewmembers we have encountered are calling you 'Padre.'"

"I guess you are right," Viktor admitted. "But let's play some chess now," he suggested.

"Absolutely," Adelheid agreed while they returned to their seats in front of the chess table.

CHAPTER 11

There was a storm in the forecast. Dark clouds on the horizon were moving swiftly, although in the opposite direction from the course of the vessel. It should not be too bad for the passengers, although advice came over the public address system to leave the deck area should lightning occur.

"Let's just leave now," Adelheid suggested to her newfound friend. "Well, let's just walk toward the other side of the ship to… starboard," she proudly announced.

"Oh yes, starboard," Viktor now corrected himself. "Let's check out some of the areas we haven't seen yet."

It was too early to take supper, so they had to decide whether to watch a movie that had been announced earlier or just wander around. They reached the deck area, where an outdoor bar with tall stools was located that was, or so it seemed to Adelheid, a busy place. Folk in beach attire and bathing suits were gathered around, waiting their turn to be served or to find an empty stool.

"How you all doin'?" a woman greeted Adelheid and Viktor as they paced their way past them.

"Very well, thank you," Adelheid and Viktor announced in unison.

"Hey! Won't you all join us for a while?" the woman offered, pointing toward a couple of empty deck chairs.

Sally and Billy, as they had introduced themselves earlier when they were table neighbors during lunch, were newlyweds.

151

Americans. Obligingly, Adelheid and Viktor accepted the offer, although with reluctance. Earlier at lunchtime Adelheid had noticed that both of them had a liking for alcohol. Only now it was beginning to show its effects.

"Will there be anything else, sir?" the steward asked Billy.

Billy looked at Adelheid and Viktor. "Anything for you folks?" he asked with a thick Texas drawl.

Adelheid and Viktor—though long ago—had both studied English. But years had passed since then and opportunities to use it were few and far between, so they had difficulty understanding either of the Americans, Sally especially, since by now her speech had become somewhat impaired due to her indulgence in alcohol.

"No, thank you," Viktor declined quickly, waving off the steward.

Billy and Sally were on their honeymoon. A wedding present from Sally's father. They were both from Texas. Sally was a spoiled "Daddy's girl," as she described herself. But a "rich Daddy's girl" would have fit her better. For Daddy was—what else? —in the oil business.

Billy, however—well, that was another story. He studied economics, as he explained earlier. He did not hold a job. And why should he? He married a "rich Daddy's girl."

But Sally was madly in love with him, and even though her rich daddy had had his doubts about Billy's true intentions, he wanted Sally to be happy. And so he gave his blessings over the whole matter.

"Was that a raindrop I just felt?" Adelheid said mostly to herself as her eyes scanned the now darkening sky.

"Indeed it was," Viktor confirmed as he wiped off a drop from his forehead.

This was a good time to excuse themselves and get away from a couple who were not exactly what one would call suitable acquaintances. At least not for Viktor and Adelheid. Not that the generation gap would have mattered. Why, Adelheid enjoyed being around young folks. That is why she studied to become a teacher. But it never came to that. She met Otto von Schleppmeister and got married instead.

As for Viktor, having been a parish priest for many years, he had dealt with young people all his life. He performed countless weddings and gave valuable advice to those in need of a mentor. But these two people?—Well, perhaps this is what they do for a hobby, drinking until....

"Have a nice evening you all!" Sally waived as Adelheid and Viktor departed rather hurriedly.

CHAPTER 12

Captain Vittorio Demarco looked up from the piece of paper he had been handed by one of the men from the communications room. "When did this message arrive?" he wanted to know.

"Just now, sir," the young man answered.

"Did anyone else see it?" the captain asked.

"No, sir. Just me—I thought it might be of some importance, that's why I wanted you to know about it right away," he added.

"I appreciate this very much," the captain complemented the young man, a fairly new crewmember and a former merchant marine.

"I would appreciate it even more," the captain continued, "if you let the contents of this message not be known to anyone else."

"My lips are sealed, sir," the sailor smiled, and with a casual salute he left the bridge.

Captain Demarco again read the contents of a small piece of paper in his hands. "We hereby inform you that an investigative team of our agency will be boarding your vessel at its next port of call. We have reason to believe that a certain amount of counterfeit currency has been traced to persons who by their own admission were recent passengers of the cruise ship Fortuna. Be prepared to accommodate the agents, for their investigation might by all estimates last through the rest of your journey."

There was a name attached, presumably the person who initiated this message, or perhaps the head of the agency, the Secret Service of the United States of America.

"This can't be happening," the captain blurted out. "Not on *my* ship!" he hissed.

"I'm sorry, sir. Did you say something?" The man on the other side of the wheelhouse wanted to know.

"Can you take over?" the captain asked his first mate. And with that he left the bridge to seek out his private quarters.

"No need for anyone to see me right now," he decided. His state of mind was in disarray, to say the least. But there was nothing he could do for now. He had to wait until the next morning, when they entered their next port of call. He sat in silence behind his huge oak desk, not really being able to concentrate on any particular duties, when a knock on the door startled him. Quickly, he removed the small piece of paper lying before him and deposited it into the breast pocket of his uniform.

"Enter!" he commanded.

It was the sailor from the communications room again, another slip of paper in his hands. "They told me I could find you here," he said apologetically. "I hope I didn't disturb you," he added.

"More bad news?" the captain asked with a frown.

"I'm not sure, sir," the sailor answered as he handed him the paper. Quickly, he left the room.

"Be aware that our agents will be dressed as 'tourists' so as not to arouse any suspicions," the paper read.

"Well, that's a relief!" The captain smiled to himself. In his mind, he had pictured a group of men in dark suits and sunglasses boarding his ship, which would surely have caused concern for the rest of his passengers.

"They will let themselves be known to you," the rest of the message read. Again, there was the signature and a few numbers beneath **it.**

Probably the badge number of this individual, he figured as he again used his breast pocket to stow away the note.

CHAPTER 13

"There is trouble on the horizon," Salvatore informed his brother, Antonio. "Not out there, dimwit!" he lectured in a hushed voice as he noticed Antonio's eyes scanning the distant sky.

"What do you mean, then?" Antonio asked angrily, a little dismayed by his brother's treatment. Wasn't it *he* who plotted their scheme? *He* who had gotten hold of that metal contraption that was once used as a prop in a movie? A contraption that turned out to be a discarded printing machine? He'd been an assistant to the prop master and thus in charge of the prop room.

Antonio had dreams back then. Dreams that he would be discovered and become a movie star. When his dreams never materialized, he decided to make use of his formal training and returned to the bank he once worked for. But then an ad in an international newsmagazines announced that interviews were being conducted for possible employment with a cruise line. Antonio jumped at the opportunity and was fortunate enough to be hired. And with his banking background he became the assistant to the head purser, the man in charge of the money.

It wasn't long afterward that Salvatore, Antonio's twin brother, was informed by his boss that he was closing his restaurant and retiring. Salvatore was also hired by the cruise line to become part of the wait staff.

THE ADVENTURES OF COUNTESS VON SCHLEPPMEISTER

"I mean," Salvatore continued as pearls of perspiration appeared on his forehead, "I mean, *we* are in trouble. In big trouble," he repeated while wiping his forehead with his handkerchief.

"Tell me," Antonio urged him, concern in his voice.

"Not here," Salvatore advised, "we might be overheard. I'll tell you all about it in our quarters tonight."

"Hey young man? Did you forget us?" A voice came from behind. It was Sally who sat nearby patiently waiting for a replenishment of her favorite drink, a Tom Collins.

"I am sorry, Madam," Salvatore apologized as he lowered the tray to set a drink before her.

"I wanted to save you a trip," she announced as she reached for the second glass which Salvatore had placed across from her. "My Billy is still asleep," she volunteered when she realized that Salvatore had assumed the second drink to be for her husband.

CHAPTER 14

*L*idia had heard enough. Enough to know that at least two crewmembers were involved in a scheme that was yet to be unraveled. She did not know them, at least not yet. But this wouldn't be a problem. All she had to do was find an excuse or a reason to approach them and take a quick look at their nametags, which each crewmember was required to wear.

But for right now, a quick glance at her surroundings assured Lidia that no one was watching as she pushed a small button on a bracelet adorning her right wrist. A tiny wire, which tangled over the railing, swiftly disappeared into the hollows of it. The small gadget attached to its end was now in Lidia's hands.

"I just love these little gadgets," she smiled to herself as she made her way back to her cabin. Once there, she deposited the tiny tape cartridge into a tape player and began to listen. Now she knew for certain that the two men she had eavesdropped on were indeed to be put under surveillance. But crooks as they might be, they were most likely lying low to avoid being discovered, and a wrong move on their part could take some time. Pretty soon the American agents would board the ship and the "catch 'em game" would begin.

"And did you have a restful night?" Viktor inquired after greeting Adelheid at their breakfast table.

"I did indeed, Viktor, and thank you for your concern." They were the first ones to arrive at the Bistro.

"You must have gotten used to the noise that kept you awake the first night," Viktor commented as he stirred the cup of tea in front of him.

"It's funny you should ask," Adelheid began, "but I haven't heard it since.""Hmm," Viktor wondered. "Well, I'm glad you are enjoying your journey as I most certainly am," he smiled. "I am really glad I met you, Adelheid, for who else would put up with an old geezer like me"

Adelheid frowned. "You must not call yourself an old— what did you call yourself?" she inquired, never having heard this expression before.

"Geezer," Viktor repeated. "An old geezer."

"Where on earth did you pick up such a word?" Adelheid wanted to know."Why, right here on the ship," he laughed. "I don't think it was supposed to reach my ears, as I am pretty sure it was pertaining to my person," he concluded."And what makes you think that?" Adelheid asked.

"Because...," he paused, "because of our acquaintances, Sally and Billy...," he paused again.

"What about Sally and Billy" Adelheid persisted.

"I don't think we should consider ourselves their friends," he continued. Viktor was struggling with words as he tried to convey what else he had overheard. Should he tell Adelheid what they called her? "The old witch who…." He never did hear much of the rest of their conversation, but from what he could pick up, he concluded that it had something to do with a comment Adelheid had made to the couple about their indulgence in liquor at all hours of the day.

But Adelheid, being the feisty lady that she was, did not give up. "Would you please tell me what is going on, Viktor? I need to know," she begged.

When Viktor finally told her the rest of what he had overheard, she was stunned. "An old witch, eh?" She grinned. But now that she was aware of the couple's feelings toward her, she was almost relieved, for she too felt an aversion toward them. They were hillbillies with money, nothing more. No class whatsoever. But why should she care? There were hundreds of people on this ship. She could choose with whomever she wants to get acquainted.

"These are really good croissants," Viktor commented as he reached for another one in the basket before him.

Adelheid, still a little dazzled over what she'd just heard, was only halfway listening. "Yes they are, indeed," she agreed, even though she had not yet touched any of the food in front of her. The cup of peppermint tea that she chose over coffee was piping hot and she almost burned her lips as she brought it to her mouth.

"Be careful! It's really hot," Viktor warned her, for he too had chosen tea this morning.

Adelheid's mind was working in high gear. She was certain that there was something going on that was not supposed to be going on. And yet, she could not put a finger on it. It was her keen sense and her sharp mind that told her to be on the lookout. But for what? Was she imagining things?

CHAPTER 16

There was again hustle and bustle aboard the Fortuna. It was the day of the cruise's second port of call in a mid-sized town along the Adriatic Sea. The first port of call two days earlier took place toward the end of the day. Perhaps deliberately so, for the town was known for its nightlife, with casinos and taverns too numerous to count. Adelheid and Viktor, however, had opted to stay on board.

But this second port had much to offer—at least according to the brochure—so she and Viktor decided the evening before to check it out. Among other things, the town was home to a small Catholic church, where one of Viktor's old friends, Father Dominique, was supposedly presiding over its parish.

The passengers were beginning to line up on the deck for debarkation. Almost everyone had a camera hanging around their neck. Some even held what Viktor described to Adelheid as video cameras. When she admitted never having heard of such a thing, Viktor smiled. "Well, you really are living 'behind the moon.'"

"Would you mind taking our picture?" came a voice from behind them. Viktor turned. Two young women holding a camera came closer.

"Don't mind if I do," Viktor volunteered. "But better yet," he turned toward Adelheid, "this lady is much better with such things," he assured them.

Adelheid gladly obliged. She had done it many times back home, when tourists wanted their picture taken in front of the Schloss Malvino, the name her castle had been given when it was used as the backdrop for a movie.

In the end, Adelheid and Viktor were almost the last ones to enter the gangplank leading to the plaza where vendors and panhandlers were wandering around in hopes of getting hold of some of the passenger's money, whether by selling "genuine" phony designer wristwatches or by just holding out hats in hopes of receiving a coin or two for the next meal.

There also were other people standing near the bottom of the gangplank. Tourists, one might assume, from their attire and the small pieces of luggage each of them had hanging over their shoulders. But instead of having just left the ship, they were actually waiting to board it.

Adelheid's mind started to work again. Instinctively, she turned to look up the gangplank she and Viktor had just left. And there, standing as if waiting for someone, was none other than the captain himself. This, Adelheid was certain, was no coincidence. These people, tourists or not, were here for a reason, and Adelheid was determined to find out what it was.

CHAPTER 17

*S*alvi, as Antonio called his brother, was patiently awaiting his brother's arrival in their shared living quarters. He was soon to be off duty as a new shift was about to begin and another assistant to the head purser was to take over.

Finally the door opened and Antonio entered. His ever-present smile turned into a frown. There was a woman sitting on one of the bunks. Maria, Salvi's "girlfriend." Fraternizing among crewmembers was discouraged.

"What is *she* doing here?" Antonio demanded in a somewhat arrogant tone of voice. "She, my dear brother…" Salvi began, but then turned toward the woman. "Here," he began again while pointing toward Maria's hands. "Why don't you just show him?" Maria got up to walk toward Antonio, who had settled into one of the chairs. Wordlessly she handed him the notes.

"We hereby inform you…" Antonio began to read out loud, but quickly stopped to read the rest in silence. His face turned white and pearls of sweat began to show as he finished, only to read the message once more.

"Where did you get these?" he asked Maria without looking up. Maria was working in the laundry and dry-cleaning shop of the ship. It was there, she explained, that she found the two notes in one of the breast pockets of the captain's uniform.

167

Antonio hissed a swarm of swear words. He had to think fast. "They must be on board by now," he figured, referring to the team of investigators mentioned in the notes. But how would they know who they were? They hadn't gotten even slightly acquainted with the entire manifest. The ship could accommodate nearly eight hundred passengers; though, this being the off-season, the vessel was booked to only two-thirds of capacity. There were unoccupied cabins on nearly every level of the ship.

"We have to clear the cabin," Antonio advised. "We've got to get rid of the evidence," he continued in a hushed voice. "Even if it means throwing it overboard."

By "evidence," Antonio was referring to the "metal contraption" that for all intents and purposes was a printer. But this was no ordinary printer. This one printed currency. American dollars, no less, and lots of them.

Antonio, in his capacity as a purser, had access to monies from all over the world. Passengers, especially Americans, carried dollars, but many also carried traveler's checks. Abroad, where currency exchange could be confusing, many Americans opted simply to pay with American dollars. And in most cases, businesses as well as hotels and restaurants actually preferred being paid in dollars. For a purser, what was easier than converting a traveler's check into phony money and pocketing the real stuff, of which the purser's vault held thousands?

From experience Antonio knew that the tourists preferred smaller denominations. Tens and twenties rather than fifties or one hundred dollar bills. So it was twenties that this printer spewed out, one by one. When they were gone, a new batch was printed. But never too many. No need to arouse suspicion. Carefully, they were dispensed with some real bills and by day's end Antonio would regularly acquire a nice bundle of the real thing.

CHAPTER 18

When Maria left the brothers' quarters, she quickly returned to her own cabin, which she shared with two co-workers—Sophia, somewhat older than Maria, and her daughter, Leni. They both had decided to sign on as washerwomen, as one would have called them in their native Austria. Sophia was a widow, and Leni a newly divorced woman. "We just wanted to see the world," they had told Maria, who was surprisingly well-versed in German. They got along fine, not just as roommates but also as friends on their off-duty time.

"Are you all right?" Sophia wanted to know when she saw tears streaming down Maria's face.

Maria did not answer. Instead, she searched for a handkerchief in her skirt pocket.

"My God, Maria! What happened?"

Maria, while still wiping tears, looked for a chair. Should she tell them what just took place? That she, Maria, naïve as she was, had just become—albeit unknowingly—an accessory to a crime that could only end in…? "Well, I cannot keep this to myself," she decided. She must tell them.

And so it was that Sophia and Leni had also become accessories, for they, too, decided to keep quiet about what they'd just heard. Did the note Maria found not say that an investigative team was to board the ship? Let them figure out who the crooks are, they decided. And with that they

171

dropped the subject. Maria, however, was still crying as she sought out the comfort of her bunk, where she eventually cried herself to sleep.

CHAPTER 19

C aptain Vittorio Demarco's meeting with the newly arrived "tourists" was brief. There was no need to arouse suspicion. He had asked the four agents, two men and two women, to avoid contact with him as much as possible, except to join him at the Captain's Table in the Lounge. There, passengers were given a chance to dine with the ship's "Master," as he was affectionately called by his crew. Meanwhile, the captain recruited his confidant, the young man from the communications room, to serve as his liaison with the agents.

"Captain, sir," Alfredo Norres promised, his right hand on his chest, "as God is my witness, you can count on me." This was good enough for the captain. He knew he could trust the young man. So, after a few instructions about how they should go about their secret plan, they parted.

Alfredo was to perform his regular duties, conveying messages that came over the wires, delivering them to either personnel or passengers, which pretty much was a daily routine. However, messages by certain "tourists" that were addressed to a certain "Mario Gillette," who in reality was the captain's long deceased brother-in-law, were to be hand-delivered to the captain.

The "tourist/agents" could only send such messages when Alfredo was on duty. Absolutely no one else was to receive them.

CHAPTER 20

Maria did not pay much attention to the man who was watching her. He was unknown to her, a passenger, like everyone else. But when he repeatedly popped up out of nowhere, she began to wonder, *Do I know this man?* In a way, he reminded her of Roberto, her old boyfriend from back home. But Roberto would never take a cruise on a ship. He had no money for such luxuries. Besides, Roberto had raven-black hair. This man's hair was reddish-blonde, with eyebrows to match. And he wore glasses—and had a mustache.

A shudder fell over Maria. *What if it is him, Roberto? Disguised with bleached hair?* Maria's fears became even stronger when she heard his voice as he spoke to one of the passengers. He did not see Maria then, for she, after noticing him, quickly hid behind a nearby door.

She was certain now that it was Roberto. But why the disguise? Why the mustache, the glasses, the bleached hair? Unless… "Oh dear God!" Maria whispered in shock. "What is he up to?" She had to find out if it really *was* Roberto. Perhaps it was just coincidence that he looked a little like Roberto—and even sounded a little like her former love. But how did he find out where she was? Did Anna, her girlfriend back home, break her promise to keep silent? Perhaps Roberto had forced her to tell him Maria's whereabouts. She only once had written to her, told her about Salvi, the new *amore* in her life.

Again, a shudder fell over Maria. This must be it, she surmised. He must have threatened Anna, or he, the ever so sweet-talking Roberto, persuaded her to give away her secret.

She must find out. She had to find a way to regain her peace of mind by knowing whether this man really was Roberto.

The opportunity arose sooner than she had hoped. Just as she was about to leave her hiding place to continue delivering dry cleaned garments to the cabins, she heard the man speak again. "My name is José, José Antruzzio," he introduced himself to one of the passengers.

A sigh of relief came over Maria, but only for a moment. What if he is using a phony name? Should she notify her superior? Tell him about her suspicions? Her fears that Roberto might harm her out of revenge for being dumped by her?

But Leonardo, the foreman in the laundry, had no ear for laments. "Sob stories," as he called them. "Don't bother me with your personal problems," he would say whenever someone was trying to find sympathy in their moments of despair.

So, Maria said nothing. "It's better this way," she decided, for she might get in trouble for even mentioning the matter. If it *is* Roberto, and if he is a legitimate passenger, he has every right to be on the ship. Disguise or no disguise.

CHAPTER 21

"*W*here is Maria?" the foreman of the laundry service asked Maria's roommates.

"I—I don't know," Sophia answered, startled. "We thought she was already here." Then with a sudden move, her hand touching her mouth as if to stop herself from speaking, she looked at Leni, who also seemed worried.

"Is anything wrong, girls?" the foreman asked.

"We… we don't know," Leni now spoke. Then, "Perhaps she went to the dispensary; she didn't feel very good last night. She might be sick."

A quick check with the ship's doctor's office came up negative. The foreman, though a little annoyed, did not react as the two women did. His only concern was that, with one person short, the rest of the laundry crew had to work harder to get their workload finished on time.

Sophia and Leni had trouble concentrating on their chores. It was Leni's turn to man the counter this morning where passengers dropped off their laundry. It was already mid-morning and still no sign of Maria. Leni noticed that Leonardo the foreman was spending more time than usual on the phone. At least one of the calls was with the captain. Leni was able to pick up bits and pieces over the noise coming from the large presses whenever the steam-pedal was activated.

"Yes, Captain, certainly, sir, I will let you know when she shows up," he assured the captain.

Leni's worries became stronger as the hours passed. "Dear God. Please let Maria be alright," she silently prayed, "let her be...."

"Good morning," a friendly voice interrupted Leni's thoughts. An elderly lady had entered the customer section of the laundry where a drop-off and pick-up counter was located. "I spilled some tea on my sweater this morning," the lady said. "I hope you can remove the stain."

"Your name, please?" Leni asked as she filled out the ticket. "Schleppmeister. Adelheid Schleppmeister," the lady repeated.

"Would you like to have it delivered to your cabin, Madam?" Leni asked.

"Oh no," Adelheid quickly replied. "A little walk will do me good," she added. The laundry was tucked away in the aft of the ship. Adelheid noticed the red around the Leni's eyes. "Are you all right, young lady?"

Leni could no longer hold back her tears. "It's Maria," she sniffed. "Maria, my roommate, she—she is missing!" she now cried out loud.

Adelheid was all ears and tried to console the young woman. "I'm sure she will be alright," she lied. Then, as fast as her feet could carry her, she disappeared, leaving Leni sobbing uncontrollably.

"We've got work to do," Adelheid greeted Viktor after arriving at their usual meeting place, the deck area with the chaise lounges and small tables. Viktor looked surprised. He didn't know what to make of her statement. But the look on Adelheid's face told him she meant business. "Let's go to my cabin," she suggested in a low voice. "It's not safe to talk around here."

Viktor, still a little startled, did not ask any questions. Wordlessly, he followed Adelheid to her cabin. Once there, she informed him that they were about to become involved in solving—or at least assisting in—a case of a missing person.

Chapter 22

$\mathscr{A}$gent Warren Howell had just left the service window in the Communications Room, where he'd dropped off a message for "Mario Gillette." The man behind the window discreetly deposited it into his pants pocket. Now he had to find an opportunity to get away from his post, to—as previously arranged —deliver it to the captain's quarters. The chance arose soon enough. A message came over the wires, addressed to all vessels at sea, that a body floating in the water had been picked up by a small fishing boat.

"Advise your crew to perform a headcount," the message continued. "This means a drill is in order," the captain acknowledged after Alfredo handed him the message. A drill usually meant all passengers had to return to their cabins, where personnel would check on them, thereby confirming that all are present and accounted for.

Suddenly, while instructing Alfredo on what was to take place, the captain stopped in mid-sentence. "The phone call!" he remembered. The call from the foreman of the laundry. "One of his workers did not show up for work and was nowhere to be found."

Vittorio Demarco had no choice but to let Alfredo in on his suspicions. He had earlier come to realize that the messages he first received from Alfredo, the ones informing him of some counterfeit money being traced to his ship, were in the breast pocket of one of the uniforms he had left with the laundry. Upon its return, however, the pockets were empty.

Inquiries about the notes would not be wise. His only hope was that whoever removed them had discarded them. Since they were in English, he had further hoped that no one would bother to translate their contents.

He now realized that he'd been wrong. The notes were found and must have fallen into the wrong hands. How? He had to find out. He proceeded to instruct Alfredo what their next move was going to be. "I need to speak to those roommates of that missing woman, Maria. I will call the foreman to let him know so he can replace them with some people from the nightshift."

"Very well, sir," Alfredo acknowledged. "Where do you want them to…?"

"Bring them right here to my quarters," the captain instructed. The captain's quarters consisted of three rooms. One was his work room or office, the other two his private quarters, complete with a small dining room, a bedroom and a bath. A small bar was tucked into the corner of the dining room, although it was rarely used since the captain was not one to indulge much in alcohol. But occasional visitors, VIPs, had been offered some of its inventory. There was bourbon, two kinds of rum, and even some Chianti. Assorted glasses, each type meant for a certain type of drink, completed the bar's inventory. A small refrigerator with an even smaller compartment for ice was built into the bar counter.

Even though the visitor who just left was no VIP, per se, in the eyes of the captain, Alfredo was indeed a "very important person." So, a drink was in order. A small jigger was filled with some bourbon and with one gulp the captain emptied its contents, not so much to acknowledge his just-departed VIP, but mostly to calm his nerves.

CHAPTER 23

The message addressed to "Mario Gillette" that Alfredo delivered, together with the message about a body having been picked up by a fishing boat, was still lying on the captain's desk where he'd completely forgotten about it. Quickly, he unfolded it to read its contents.

What will it be this time? he wondered. *More bad news perhaps?* His eyes scanned the piece of paper: "We have identified possible suspects, and are continuing to watch their activities. We'll keep you informed of further developments." A pre-arranged codename was signed on the bottom of the paper. Even though Vittorio Demarco was somewhat relieved after reading the "good news," he was equally disappointed that no names of the possible suspects were given. *Well, I'm sure they know what they are doing,* he concluded. *It's all in their hands now. But what about Maria?* he wondered.

He picked up the phone to dial the Communications Room. A voice that he recognized as not being that of Alfredo, his confidante, answered. Quickly he returned the phone to its cradle. *I'll have to try again later,* he decided. The agents needed to be informed about the body that had been picked up and that a crewmember was reported missing. If there was a connection, then foul play could not be ruled out.

CHAPTER 24

As it turned out, there was no need for the captain to inform the agents about Maria's disappearance, nor of the possibility that it was her body that had been plucked from the water by a fisherman. The agents had already received such news from another source: the Italian contingent of the Secret Service. Lidia Frattera, who'd earlier helped Adelheid out of her deck chair, had again run into her just as she was about to drop off a garment at the laundry to be pressed. "What's your hurry, Ma'am?" she smiled.

Adelheid looked up. "Oh, Lidia, right?" she asked to assure herself of having addressed the women by her correct name.

"That's right," the woman confirmed. "Lidia Frattera— and what was your name again?"

"Oh I'm so sorry, Lidia," Adelheid smiled apologetically. "I thought you knew." She was lying since she knew full well that she'd never given Lidia her name at their initial encounter. "It's Adelheid—just call me Adelheid." And with that she was about to leave when she remembered Lidia's question. What was her hurry? she wanted to know. Adelheid could not help but divulge what she had just been told about one of the washerwomen gone missing.

"Really?" Lidia now listened up.

"That's all I know," Adelheid assured her, aware of Lidia's eagerness to hear more. "Ask the young woman behind the counter," she went on and pointed at the laundry room. "She is her roommate"

"Or perhaps, *was* her roommate," Adelheid said more to herself than to Lidia, who was already disappearing behind the door of the laundry room.

Leni went on writing notes on Adelheid 's ticket as Lidia waited her turn. Another customer had entered before Lidia, and Leni, after checking the ticket stub handed to her, disappeared behind a row of racks and pressed a control button that set the racks into motion until the correct garment came into sight. Before Leni returned to the counter, Lidia had a chance to look at Adelheid's ticket, still lying on the counter. A quick glance told her that Adelheid was Adelheid Schleppmeister. Countess Adelheid von Schleppmeister.

Lidia was excited. Earlier, she had wondered where she had seen the old woman before. Now she remembered. A photo in a news article she'd seen not long before. Adelheid was the woman who had played a role in the recovery of some jewels heisted years earlier—far too many years ago for Lidia to have known the details of the actual robbery. Fourteen years earlier she was just finishing school as a freshman and hadn't even decided on a career yet, but now, as an agent of a certain law-enforcement agency, she knew about the theft and later recovery of the jewels. Her agency and most other international agencies kept each other informed about major cases. Besides, the news media made sure that the rest of the world knew.

Exchanging a few words with Leni, Lydia hoped to learn more about the woman's missing roommate. But a voice in the back of the laundry summoned Leni, and another worker took over the counter service. Lidia left the laundry. Once outside, her hand reached into the pocket of her shorts. A faint click turned off the tape recorder that she'd activated earlier.

CHAPTER 25

The captain's rooms were slowly filling with people. Seven to be exact, himself included. He had summoned them ever so carefully, one by one, to arrive at his quarters. There were two male agents with their female partners, who posed as their "wives"; Lidia, their counterpart from Rome; and Alfredo, the young man from the radio room. There were two more scheduled to arrive. Captain Demarco checked his watch just as another knock on the door announced the arrival of the last participants of this clandestine rendezvous.

"Sorry for being late," Sophia apologized in her native German. She was too embarrassed to try out what little knowledge she had of the Italian language.

"Keine Endschuldigung noetig," the Captain responded, answering in almost flawless German. He was quite versed in several languages—almost a prerequisite for a man in his position. Over the years he had met people from all over the world and along the way adopted their language. He was hardly fluent in all of them, but enough so to engage in conversations that related to his duties.

"As long as you weren't seen by anyone," he continued, "that's all that…"

"Oh no! No one saw us coming," Sophia assured the captain.

"Well then, let's get started," the captain suggested, his eyes scanning the room for more chairs. "Let's sit in here." He pointed toward the dining room, where exactly eight chairs surrounded the oval table. One short. He pushed his desk chair in front of him, placing it at the head of the table.

"I believe introductions are in order?" he asked as his eyes met with each of his guests'. Everyone obliged by stating their name and why they were present. Then one by one they revealed what they had learned so far. After Sophia and Leni stated what they knew, how Maria had confided in them about what she had witnessed in Salvatore and Antonio's quarters, they were certain it was Maria's body that had been recovered from the sea.

"She just knew too much," Sophia sobbed. Leni tried to console her mother, but to no avail. After having been sworn to secrecy, the two women were excused. The rest of the group began to lay out its next move.

"We need someone," Agent Howell began to speak, "someone who could...." He hesitated before he continued. "We need someone who could spy for us without ever being suspected. Someone..."

"Ahem," Lidia raised her hand in excitement. "And I know just the right person for the job!" she announced enthusiastically. "In fact," she continued, "I think she is perfect for the job"

CHAPTER 26

"*You* want me to do *what?*" Adelheid blurted out after Lidia stated her request.

"Shhh, not so loud!" Lidia cautioned. She had taken a post by the entrance of the Bistro, which she had noticed was one of Adelheid's favorite places to take in her meals. "Why don't we meet later, perhaps in my quarters," Lidia suggested. "I will tell you all the details of what is going on."

"I can hardly wait!" Adelheid responded with a hint of apprehension in her voice. She'd just found out that Lidia was Agent Lidia Frattera, a member of the Secret Service, or a contingent thereof in Italy, specializing in matters pertaining to counterfeit currency. Once in Lidia's cabin, Adelheid did not have to think long about accepting Lidia's offer. Why, this was right up her alley! "Snooping—I'm in," she smiled, "but with one condition. I would like to have my friend Father Viktor be by my side while I—snoop around."

Lidia was elated over Adelheid's request. Viktor was a Catholic priest who, for at least part of his life, conducted the Mass in Latin. What language could be closer to Italian than Latin? He could be Adelheid's interpreter!

"You took the words right out of my mouth" Lidia laughed.

"Let's get Viktor," Adelheid suggested.

"What's his cabin number?" Lidia asked.

Minutes later a somewhat befuddled Viktor was sitting in a comfortable chair in Lidia's cabin. "I promise not to doze off," he smiled at Lidia, who repeatedly apologized for interrupting his afternoon nap. Before she had reached Viktor's cabin, she decided to check out the deck where she had seen Viktor and Adelheid on several occasions before. It was there where she found him, peacefully snoring on a reclining deck chair.

Nevertheless, he was all ears as Lidia began to lay out her plan. And so it was that Adelheid and her friend Viktor became a pair of full-fledged sleuths who were about to become instrumental in the apprehension of a pair of counterfeiters, of whom at least one might be a murderer.

CHAPTER 27

"*You* bastard," Salvi greeted his brother as he entered their quarters. "What did you do with her?"

"Do with who?" Antonio asked, puzzled.

"Maria!" Salvi screamed. "What did you do with Maria?!!"

Rage was showing in his face as Antonio had often seen in Salvi before, but never directed toward himself. Salvi, although not the smarter of the two, was—to say the least—the more temperamental. This was in many cases to his disadvantage. Back home in the village where they grew up, Salvi had occasional run-ins with the law, mainly for losing his temper, which usually ended up in a fistfight with whoever got in his way. He even spent a night in jail once for just such an incident.

That was many years ago, when they were both very young and sometimes a little too boisterous, leaving them with not too many friends. As a result, the villagers dubbed them "the fighting twins." Once they were old enough to leave home they decided to seek life in the big city.

Antonio took on an apprenticeship as a bank-teller. He had some training already, mostly from classes in accounting at a nearby vocational school. He'd always been fascinated by money. Even as a child, he would cut pieces of paper into shapes of currency. Then, with color crayons, he would adorn them with numbers to depict their denominations. With an innocence only a child could possess, he would visit the local grocer to "buy" some candies. The grocer knew Antonio well, for his mother was one of his customers. "Just put it on my bill," she would instruct him, and the grocer would always oblige Antonio's wishes by "selling" him some candies, which the man did not, in fact, always put on the mother's bill. Instead, he was more concerned about Antonio's behavior. There was a streak of larceny in his character that could someday get him into something much worse than passing off "play money."

Salvi was not quite as ambitious as Antonio. He had no interest in furthering his education. Instead, he became a waiter. Waiters make good tips, especially in restaurants and hotels that catered to tourists. He, however, ended up in a small bistro mostly frequented by locals. When the owner decided to retire, Salvi asked Antonio to get him a job with the cruise line. It was mostly luck that had him end up on the same vessel as his brother, an assistant purser.

CHAPTER 28

*A*ntonio was genuinely surprised to hear about Maria's disappearance. "Liar!" Salvi had called him. "You liar!" But Antonio swore on their mother's grave, "I did not touch her!" Salvi was not so sure. They both were aware that Maria—after having found those messages in the captain's uniform pockets—had come to realize that the brothers were involved in a dreadful crime. The possibility of her informing the authorities was indeed on their minds. So it would be logical to silence the mouth that might give them away. But again, Antonio pleaded innocence.

After Salvi's anger had subsided a little, he sat down. Now they had to plot their next move. "We've got to try to at least print one more batch," Antonio began. "I've got enough paper to make up at least several hundred of twenties."

By "paper" he meant the special paper that is used for printing currency. And by "twenties" he was of course talking about dollars. Good old American dollars.

"No!" Salvi warned. "It's... it's just too risky. Let's just be satisfied with what we have," he said, hoping to dissuade Antonio.

Antonio rose from his chair to walk toward the built-in wardrobe. A large cache was hidden in a safe behind some clothing. Slowly, he turned the dial. First left, then right, then left again. He reached for one of the bundles of bills—the real bills—and slowly brought them to his lips. "I love you," he smiled as he caressed this so-precious commodity.

"We've got to get rid of this," Salvi warned, watching his brother return the bundle into the strongbox.

Antonio agreed. "But let's just print up one more batch and then find a safe hiding place for it—and the printer, too," he said.

Cabin twenty-four was no longer a safe place to hide the printer. Antonio had, as did most of the crewmembers, passkeys to certain areas. This was how he acquired the key to cabin twenty-four. Periodically, the brothers would, in the middle of the night, visit twenty-four to replenish their supply of phony bills, which they would then exchange for the real ones.

"Let's go," Antonio motioned to Salvi as he walked toward the door, a rolled up bathrobe under his arm.

"Where to?" Salvi wanted to know.

"Do you need to ask?" Antonio answered, a little annoyed. "We've got to visit a certain cabin," he announced. "And— and if we are seen—we are just going for a swim," he smiled, pointing to the bundle under his arm. "Better take yours, too." Salvi obliged and together they left their quarters to attend matters in cabin twenty-four.

CHAPTER 29

*A*delheid sat up in bed. She rubbed her eyes while trying to read the numbers on the illuminated clock by her bedside. It was a little after midnight. A noise had awakened her, but it now had subsided. Just as she turned over to resume her sleep—there it was again. A slight rumble coming from the cabin next door. It was the same kind of noise she had heard the first night. Back then she had assumed that it was coming from the vessel's engines, but when she never heard it again, she just forgot about the whole matter.

Thump, thump, came from behind the walls of her bed. And again—*thump, thump.* Should she summon Viktor? Have him listen? But no, she wouldn't dare awaken him, perhaps even worry him. *Over what? A noise behind the wall? How silly of me,* she thought. And with that she rolled over to resume her sleep, noise or no noise.

The next morning, passing the cabin next to hers, she glanced at its number. "Twenty-four" the brass plate read.

CHAPTER 30

*L*idia, as decided at their clandestine meeting in the Captain's quarters, was to be Adelheid and Viktor's table partner at their usual place in the Bistro. This was the most inconspicuous way for them to communicate and pass on observations. Things the older woman and Viktor would pick up by watching certain crewmembers who by now had been pretty much identified as suspicious earlier, when Lidia secretly taped a conversation by two crewmembers who turned out to be brothers. Twin brothers, in fact, who looked exactly alike.

But they still needed proof. Proof of them being the ones involved in passing counterfeit money. Certainly, the circumstances were perfect. Antonio, the assistant purser, who had access to real money. Money that could be switched with the phony stuff.

Then there was the disappearance of Maria, who was Salvi's girlfriend. She, who had given them the messages she had found. Maria, who was missing and whose body had been positively identified as the one fished from the sea. The nametag, still attached to her clothing, identified her as a crewmember of the Fortuna. But were they ready to make an arrest?

"Do you carry any traveler's checks?" Lidia asked Adelheid while they were having their breakfast.

"Why, yes," Adelheid answered, picking up her purse. Lidia reached across the table to touch Adelheid's hand.

"Don't take them out," she whispered, "not here anyway."

After laying out the plot of Adelheid's first assignment, she excused herself to return to her cabin, where she was to meet with the American agents.

CHAPTER 31

"And could you please make it twenties?" Adelheid asked the purser behind the window.

"Madam is planning a trip to America?" the purser asked, curious as to why this little old lady would request American dollars instead of European currency.

Adelheid, not prepared for such a question, had to come up with an answer without arousing any suspicion of the real reason for her transaction. "Oh no," she lied. "But you see, there is this couple I met. Americans on their honeymoon," she chuckled. "They bought a clock at the last port of call but decided that it was too much bother to take it on in their luggage, so I offered to buy it from them."

"We have postal service on the ship," the purser informed her. "They could mail it back home," he suggested.

Adelheid again had to come up with a quick reply. "But I really want that clock!" she continued on with the lie. "You see, it's an antique clock, and I just love antiques, especially clocks. And besides, it's a bargain."

"I see," the purser replied as he counted out the bills into Adelheid's hands. "Twenty, forty, sixty...."

CHAPTER 32

"*B*oy, that was close," Adelheid commented when she and Viktor met again with Lidia at their regular table. "Viktor," Adelheid continued as she discreetly handed the twenty-dollar bills to Lidia, "if this weren't a mission, I would make you my 'Beichtvater' so you could absolve me from my sins"

Viktor smiled. "You did the right thing," he consoled her. "The lies you told that man were not lies in the eyes of God. On the contrary, they were...."

Lidia interrupted him. "I'm sorry, Padre, but I do have to leave again, duty calls, you know." She smiled.

Before her departure, she had discreetly deposited an envelope into Adelheid's purse, which rested on an empty chair beside her. "It's all there," she smiled. "The real stuff," she added as she waved a goodbye. "See you at supper," she reminded Adelheid and Viktor when she left the Bistro.

She was to meet again with the American agents, this time in their quarters. The two cabins were next to each other. One was occupied by the female agents and the other by the two men. The "husband and wife" thing was only a front. Just two couples traveling together, nothing more. By now they, too, had made the acquaintance with Sally and Billy. But, just like Adelheid and Viktor, they'd surmised that the American couple were just hopeless drunks out to spend rich daddy's money. They were of no use to the agents. The couple had enough cash on them, which Billy in particular had a habit of flaunting whenever the occasion arose. Traveler's checks were not what they carried. Perhaps a good thing, for they most likely would by now have been ripped off big time. Lidia had entered the cabin in which she was to meet with the agents.

"Any luck?" Agent Howell asked.

Without any reply, Lidia opened the envelope she had received from Adelheid. A bundle of twenties exchanged hands. Then one of the agents produced scanning gadgets, part of their "tools of their trade," as they call them.

One by one agent Warren Howell scanned each bill, and one by one they ended up on the stack of the counterfeits. Only four of the twenty-five bills turned out to be real. "That son of a bitch," the agent hissed, as he almost slammed down the last of the phony bills. "That's their game," he continued. "They rip off the unsuspecting little old ladies, like our Adelheid." The "our" was an affectionate addition to Adelheid's name because she so much reminded him of his own grandmother, who incidentally arrived in America as an immigrant many years earlier.

The angry expression on agent Howell's face turned into a smile. They now had the proof they were looking for.

Counterfeit American dollars being paid out to unsuspecting passengers in exchange for traveler's checks, which were then deposited in the vault, from which the real dollars were taken, which, instead of being paid out to the customer, disappeared into Antonio's pockets. Only one question remained—where was the rest of the evidence? The printer on which those phony bills were produced. Was it on board? Or somewhere ashore, at the home port most likely?

Without that printer their case was not complete. They had found the man who dealt with the money exchange. But was he also the one who printed the counterfeit money? What role was played by Salvatore, or Antonio? The agents had no choice. They had to find the printer.

CHAPTER 33

$\mathcal{A}$nother meeting was to take place in the Captain's quarters among the four American agents, Lidia, and the newly recruited sleuths, Adelheid and Viktor. There was not a lot to report, except that the laundry service was still short and needed a replacement for Maria. So it was decided that one of the female agents was to fill in until a permanent replacement could be taken on at the next port of call.

Nancy Riggs was no stranger to the laundry and dry-cleaning business. Back in her hometown in upstate New York, she frequently helped out in her uncle's business. This was a way to put herself through college. A scholarship awarded to her was another source, allowing her to graduate with a degree in criminal justice.

"Are you sure you want to do this?" the captain asked, a note of doubt in his voice.

"Absolutely," she smiled. "I may be a rookie agent, but I am a pro in the laundry."

"In that case," the captain announced, "you've got the job"

The main reason for Nancy's employment at the laundry was—at least in part—to keep an eye and ear open and to gather intelligence, if at all possible. After a few more details on the events that had taken place so far, Adelheid was ready to excuse herself.

"If you don't mind? I'm rather tired you know," she explained while hiding a yawn behind the palm of her hand.

"But of course," the captain assured her as he rose to help her out of a stuffed chair. "It was that noise next door again," she tried to explain.

The captain's ears perked up. "What noise was that, Madam?"

"Well…" Adelheid hesitated before she continued, "that thump, thump, thump noise coming from the cabin next to mine. Cabin number twenty-four, I believe."

Now everyone was all ears. The captain opened a desk drawer to remove the manifest, the logbook which listed the names of all passengers, where they were from, and which cabins they occupied. One glance assured him what he had already suspected. Cabin number twenty-four—"unoccupied," it read.

Then from another drawer the captain removed a small strongbox that held hundreds of keys. He reached for the one with a label attached that was marked with the letter "M." This was the most important key of them all. The letter "M" stood for "Master Key."

By now the agents were all aware of what was happening. They had solved another puzzle. They, or so they hoped, had found the whereabouts of that elusive printing device. This meant, though, they had to act fast. Should they stake out cabin number twenty-four? Perhaps lay in wait behind its door? Or should they hold out in Adelheid's cabin until that thump-thump noise started up again? It was by all accounts coming from a mechanical device, which the agents were almost certain was a printer.

"We must catch them 'in flagrante delicto," Agent Howell decided, "right in the act of printing the stuff." So, after Adelheid and Viktor departed, a more detailed plan was devised.

CHAPTER 34

Captain Demarco sat at his desk with Nancy Riggs, who remained behind after the other agents had left. "Are you sure you are up to this?" the captain asked her again as he looked up the phone number of the laundry.

"I most certainly am!" she answered enthusiastically. "After all, it's all part of my job. It's not that I..." she stopped in mid-sentence as the captain motioned with extended arms for her to be silent.

"Let me speak with Leonardo," he instructed the person who answered the phone. While drumming on the desk with his free hand, he waited eagerly for Leonardo.

A voice, loud enough for Nancy to hear, came over the line. "Yes?" It sounded somewhat short and impatient.

"This is Captain Demarco... listen, if you have a minute, could you come by my office? I would like to discuss something with you."

The voice on the other end was no longer audible to Nancy. She figured that was only because it was the captain himself on the phone that Leonardo Gambucci resorted to a more civilized tone of voice.

"Good!" The captain smiled. "See you shortly," he added as he hung up.

He turned to Nancy. "Now let's go over this once more.... You are a passenger, and because you heard of the laundry service being behind schedule due to a member of the laundry crew having fallen "ill," you are offering your expertise to help out. Okay?"

"Do you think it will wash? Eh—I mean no pun intended; does it sound believable?" Nancy asked.

"I'm sure it will work," the captain nodded.

A knock on the door announced the arrival of Leonardo. He was a typical Italian. Not tall, with black hair and deep-set dark eyes, which gave him the look of some Mafia character in the movies. His raspy voice was that of a person whose love for whiskey was evident.

After introducing Nancy by first name only, the captain informed Leonardo of his plan. "As you know, this is against company regulations. I mean involving passengers in the ship's operations, but I think we can make an exception, since I know you are hours behind schedule."

"Ah, yes," Leonardo agreed.

"And not to worry," the captain continued. "She's got plenty of experience, I assure you."

Together, Nancy and Leonardo returned to the laundry. "I'll have Sophia train you in on the procedures, the routine and such," Leonardo began in a somewhat resigned tone of voice. He was not too happy about this arrangement, behind schedule or not. "Let Sophia decide which area she wants you to work," he added.

"I can do the front counter," Nancy suggested. She remembered from one of her visits to the laundry that the phone was mounted on a nearby wall.

Leonardo gave her a startled look. It had suddenly occurred to him that she, Nancy, might just happen to understand his native tongue. She could pick up on conversations that were not meant for other ears whenever he was conducting one of his "business deals."

Not to arouse suspicion, he agreed. "Fine, but I do need you on the press, whenever there is a lunch break for the presser."

"Okay by me," Nancy agreed. She did not let on that by now she had surmised that her presence near the instrument of Leonardo's dealings, namely the telephone, was not to his liking. At the same time, she wondered if he ever was concerned about being overheard by the switchboard operator, who undoubtedly must be multilingual and thus familiar with many languages.

"Perhaps he speaks in code," she thought. A familiar face came from the rear section of the laundry. Just as Leonardo was about to introduce Nancy, Sophia had recognized her from the meeting in the captain's quarters. But with Nancy holding a finger to her lips, Sophia immediately understood.

"This is Nancy," Leonardo began as he turned toward Nancy. Sophia, not sure how to react, just nodded. "She will be helping out for a while until we find a replacement for Maria," he continued. And with that he left the two women alone to go about his work at the other end of the facility.

Sophia, still speechless at this point, looked at Nancy, who again raised a finger to her lips. "I'll tell you all about it later," she explained in a subdued voice. And then more audibly, "Okay, where do I start?"

CHAPTER 35

$\mathscr{V}$ ictor and Adelheid were on duty. They'd decided to explore more of the ship's nooks and crannies—go to areas where they might be able to observe more of the daily activities of the ship. The captain had given them permission to visit the upper deck, where only first-class passengers were allowed.

The layout was similar to that of the lower deck with the exception of the swimming pool, which was almost twice the size of the one on the lower deck. "It makes no sense," Adelheid murmured as she scanned the area that took in almost one fourth of the upper deck.

"What makes no sense, Adelheid?" Victor asked.

"The pool," Adelheid answered. "The pool," she repeated. "Why is it so much bigger when there are much fewer people on this deck?"

"It's because it's first class," Victor explained. "Don't you see? You pay more, you get more."

Adelheid just shook her head as they entered the walkway, which covered the perimeter of the pool area, to make their way to the other side. Only a few people were making use of the pool. A set of parents with some small children—only three as far as one could tell. One of them was busy teaching the smallest how to swim, while the other two were having a water fight, splashing each other and shrieking and giggling. The rest of the pool was used by a couple of young folks repeatedly swimming the length of the pool, back and forth, as if training for the Olympics.

The deck chairs were mostly empty; only a few were occupied. Perhaps it was still too early in the morning. For most of the passengers, indulging in the nightlife on such a cruise ship led to them sleeping in to recover from their previous night's activities. There was dancing in the "Lido" as well as a stage show with singers, comedians and a few wanna-be passengers who, by invitation from the activity director, climbed the stage to belt out a mostly off-key version of certain songs, earning them a mostly obligatory round of applause, perhaps even an earned one; the laughter accompanying the clapping of hands reflected the audience's pleasure in watching someone making a fool of themselves.

"Let's sit down for a while," Adelheid suggested, noticing Viktor's limp had become more distinct.

"It's my arthritis," he explained as he stopped for a minute to rest. "Here," Adelheid pointed at a nearby small table with two chairs. "Let's just sit here for a while." There was no one around to overhear them, so Adelheid began to deliberate. "I think the first thing we should do is...."

An elderly gentleman was nearing their table. He, too, was using a cane like Viktor, only his was mostly a prop. An English custom in which gentlemen, regardless of age, carry a walking stick, as they are sometimes called. Many of them convert into umbrellas—a sensible idea, since it rains a lot in Britain.

"Good morning!" the man greeted Adelheid and Viktor, who returned his greeting.

216

"Lovely morning, is it not?" he continued, slowing his pace to scan the blue horizon while one hand shielded his eyes from the sun.

"You must be an Englishman," Adelheid commented. "I mean your accent...."

"Indeed I am, Madam!" The man pivoted to face Adelheid. He removed his hat, a style mostly worn in the English countryside. "Foster Morrison at your service," he smiled.

Adelheid held out her hand. "I'm Adelheid Schleppmeister and this is Father Viktor." She pointed at Viktor, who was making an effort to rise from his chair.

"Please don't get up," the Englishman said as he noticed Viktor struggling. "It's a pleasure to m

et you both," he continued. "Although, I must confess— for a minute I thought you were a couple—I mean, husband and wife...."

"Oh, no!" Adelheid laughed. "No, we are just travel partners and friends," she explained. No need to go into details as to why they were seen together so often.

"Won't you sit down?" Adelheid offered as the Englishman looked around for a third chair.

"Don't mind if I do," he smiled as he watched Viktor using his cane to hook onto a leg of a nearby chair to pull it closer.

"So... where is home in England?" Viktor asked, hoping to initiate a conversation.

CHAPTER 36

As it turned out, Foster Morrison was no stranger to the spying business. During the war he was an officer in a British intelligence unit. After the war, he resumed his tenure as a professor at the University of Liverpool, where he taught criminal justice until he'd retired a few years ago. He had a son, who, like himself, was a member of the faculty at Liverpool, where he was teaching history.

Adelheid was very impressed by her new acquaintance. He was a man of character and prestige. He was knighted by the king after leaving the military service but did not flaunt his title. "Sir Foster" sounded a bit pretentious to him. He had come from a family of simple means. His father had lost the family's fortune during the stock market crash in 1929. But even with little money left, he'd managed to send his only son to a prestigious school.

"Well—I better be on my way," Foster Morrison excused himself, looking at his watch. "I'll have to fetch me some breakfast before they close down the buffet." He laughed and waved goodbye. "Let's get together again for a cup of tea later!" he called out.

"Indeed, we shall!" Adelheid promised.

CHAPTER 37

"What do you make of the Englishman—I mean Foster?" Viktor asked Adelheid.

"I think we should let the agents know what happened to him while he was ashore," Adelheid responded. It was during their conversation with their newly found acquaintance that he mentioned a rather embarrassing incident. He had stopped at a small restaurant to take in some refreshment, when the waiter, after receiving payment for his tab, returned to his table with the twenty dollar bill he had received from Foster still in his hand.

"I'm awfully sorry, sir," he began, "but we can no longer accept American currency."

"May I ask for the reason of this measure?" Foster asked, a little puzzled. Earlier, before he debarked the ship, he had stopped by the purser's window to exchange some English pounds for the local currency. But the purser had advised him to exchange it for American dollars instead.

"The local merchants prefer American money," he explained. The waiter hesitated while trying to find English words to explain the reason. The owner of the restaurant noticed the waiter struggling and approached the table.

"My sincere apologies, sir," he began, "but word has gotten around that phony American money is being spent along the coastline. So we can't take the risk…"

"I'm sorry to hear that," Foster replied with genuine concern. "Will you take English pounds?" he inquired.

"It will have to do," the owner replied, "but I'm not sure how much your tab would be in pounds. I would have to…."

"Just take this bill," Foster offered. "I'm certain it will cover more than what I have consumed. Consider the rest a gratuity for your inconvenience," he added as he left the establishment.

Adelheid realized now why a startled look crossed Foster's face when a waiter approached their table with an assortment of drinks on a tray. Although it was still early in the morning, there were always a few who indulged in alcoholic drinks. But mostly it was orange juice or lemonade and tomato juice, known to be a cure for hangovers from too much indulgence the night before.

"That's odd," Foster spoke more to himself after the waiter had passed their table.

"Excuse me?" Adelheid asked as if she didn't hear correctly.

"That waiter," Foster began. "I could have sworn I saw him before, but in a different capacity."

It was then they realized that he had seen Antonio at the purser's window. "He has a twin brother," Adelheid explained. "One of the pursers," she added. But having been sworn to secrecy, she could not divulge what they knew. They had to get in touch with Lidia as soon as possible.

CHAPTER 38

"When can I meet him?" Lidia asked as they sat at their usual table in the Bistro.

"He will join us shortly," Adelheid smiled. "I told him to meet us at eleven-forty-five. That way we'll have a chance to fill you in of what he told us, and then perhaps let you decide if we should tell him what is going on." "Great!" Lidia agreed.

Adelheid's eyes were fixed toward the Bistro's entrance. "Here he is now," she announced when she spotted Foster making his way toward their table. "The pleasure is all mine," Foster smiled when he was introduced to Lidia.

During lunch the conversation was minimal. The room had filled quickly and the noise level was such that a subdued conversation was impossible.

"Agent Howell is waiting for us," Lidia revealed to Adelheid, who was the first to finish her meal. After the rest of the group had finished, they all departed to make their way to Warren Howell's cabin. They never got that far. Just as they were leaving the Bistro they came upon the agent coming their way.

"The captain wants to see us," he explained. He looked at Lidia and then at Foster; before he could speak, Lidia spoke a few words, to which he just nodded.

"Enter," the captain's voice came from within. Agent Howell opened the door. He motioned to Adelheid, Lidia and Viktor to enter first, then entered with Foster and closed the door behind himself.

The captain had readied some chairs around the dining room table. "Please, sit down," he offered. Before any of them had a chance to introduce Foster to the captain, the two were shaking hands and embracing.

"Nice to see you again, old boy," Foster greeted the captain, who was elated to see his old friend.

"I had no idea you were on my ship," he laughed apologetically. "I must have missed your name when I read the manifest."

"It was a last minute decision," Foster explained. "You see, it was my son who wanted to take this cruise. But unexpected circumstances forced him to cancel, so he offered the cruise to me. Perhaps it is *his* name on the manifest."

"Well—it's great to have you aboard, my friend," the captain told him.

The group had taken their seats. Agent Howell was satisfied that Lidia was right when she had made the comment, "He is on our side," after noticing Howell's expression at the time of his introduction back at the Bistro.

"Let's get started," the captain began as he pulled his chair into position. After having related to Foster what had happened so far, he continued, "We have checked out cabin twenty-four, but could not find evidence of any sort that would relate to our suspicions."

"Are there any other unoccupied cabins that could be checked out?" Agent Howell inquired.

The captain smiled. "We have already done so." By *we* he was referring to Alfredo, his confidant, who, with the master key, had, ever so casually, entered certain unoccupied cabins to look for anything that shouldn't be there.

224

"Perhaps it is no longer on board," agent Howell concluded, referring to what they assumed to be the printer.

Two hours passed before the group ended the meeting, during which a new plan was devised and assignments were given to further their investigation.

CHAPTER 39

*N*ancy Riggs had her hands full. Not only was she overwhelmed with her assigned workload, she also had her hands full with Leni, who repeatedly broke out in tears over her missing friend. Word of Maria's demise had not reached her for the simple reason that it had not been announced to anyone thus far.

Nancy also had to keep an eye on the foreman whenever he spoke on the phone, hoping to pick up words from his conversation that might pertain to clandestine business.

"Well, I agreed to this assignment, so I might as well make the best of it," she decided. Leonardo received several calls. They were coming from a land-line, as Nancy soon discovered, for the person on the other end must have asked a certain question, to which Leonardo replied, "We should arrive there as scheduled." And then, "I'll meet you at Gino's."

Gino's, Nancy assumed, must be a tavern or restaurant somewhere at the next port of call. Nancy was surprised by how much she understood of his conversation. Her knowledge of Italian stemmed from when she was still a child. Her grandmother was a full-blooded Italian who, just like Warren Howell's grandmother, had immigrated to the United States of America. Not eager to acquire a new language, Nancy's grandma used her native tongue around the family. They in turn learned rather quickly to become bilingual. On many occasions Nancy served as her grandmother's interpreter.

She abruptly looked up while sorting a load of bed linens; bed sheets on one pile, pillow covers on another. A chambermaid had dropped them off. A sudden feeling of being watched now proved correct as she saw Leonardo standing nearby, but in a way intended to keep himself from being noticed. *Is he checking me for competence?* she wondered—or is he testing me? Testing me for what? Nancy didn't have to guess any further. A swarm of Italian words came from Leonardo's lips as he shouted over the noise of the press.

But Nancy was prepared. "Excuse me?" she asked, looking at him.

Leonardo again shouted in Italian. Nancy shrugged her shoulders and just stared at him. Finally, Leonardo repeated his words in English: "You make..." he motioned with his arms, simulating the sorting. Right, left, right, his arms moved quickly. "You make faster?" he finished his sentence.

"Oh!" Nancy acknowledged is request. Without paying any further attention to him, she continued her chore.

"You make faster," she smiled to herself.

CHAPTER 40

fter the group left the captain's quarters they all had work to do. Adelheid and Viktor were again promenading the various decks where they hoped to find what was described to them as a money-printing device. No one knew exactly what it might look like. But it probably was not too big, perhaps the size of a typewriter. It could have a drum barrel and some sort of ink dispenser. And of course a plate engraved with the likes of a twenty-dollar note: President Andrew Jackson, the seventh president of the United States of America, on one side, and a picture of the White House on the other. Perhaps there were even two plates. One for each side.

"If you should find anything—anything at all," Agent Howell instructed them, "do not touch it, but immediately let me or any of the other agents know of its whereabouts. And… have one of you stay behind, to make sure no one will remove it."

Lidia was assigned to drop off some clothing to be laundered so she could make contact with Nancy Riggs, who might have some information to be passed on that could not wait till the end of her shift. And indeed she did. But it was too risky to carry on a conversation about anything other than laundry matters, so she wrote some notes on Lidia's laundry ticket before handing it to her. Lidia nodded and quickly left the laundry.

CHAPTER 41

The rest of the agents were off on their assignments. They were to mingle with the passengers, asking casual questions that might seem unimportant but could lead to information in one way or another. Their efforts were rewarded when they met two ladies, sisters it turned out, who both were retired schoolteachers now enjoying a life of leisure. They were from Switzerland, which possesses at least three languages: "Swyzer Dütch," a dialect from the German language that is spoken but seldom written; French; and Italian.

"Excuse me," Agent Wills began as he approached the two women. "I didn't mean to eavesdrop on you, and I don't even mean to be nosy or rude... but your language ...I don't seem to recognize it."

The two women smiled, both answering at the same time, making it even more difficult to understand them.

"It is what?" Agent Wills asked again.

"It's Swiss German," one of them now said in English.

After a few minutes of small talk the agents continued their walk, but soon decided to return to the area where they had met the Swiss ladies.

"I'm curious as to what she was trying to tell us," the female agent said, speaking more to herself than her companion.

"What do you mean?" Agent Wills asked.

"Well, didn't you notice how one of them acted while the other one started to say something? She literally reached for the other's mouth as if trying to silence her."

"Well, yeah," Agent Wills agreed. "That's because they both wanted to talk at the same time."

"I don't think so. She wanted to talk about something she had observed, remember? She had mentioned that she had left their cabin during the night, to catch some fresh air. How she had admired the starlit sky"

"Yeah, so?" Agent Wills laughed. "So she likes to look at stars"

"But then," the female agent continued, "when she began to mention that she saw two men in bathing trunks, and was wondering why, since the swimming pool was closed... that's when the other one tried to shut her up."

"Maybe they were skinny-dipping," Agent Wills joked, then suddenly became serious. The swimming pool was closed, all right, but only for the passengers. At night, after midnight to be exact, it was open to the crew until four a.m. Then the maintenance crew arrived to do their job.

"Let's see if they are still there," he suggested, referring to the Swiss ladies. "Remember," he reminded the female agent, "we are Mr. and Mrs. Wills...."

CHAPTER 42

*A*fter leaving the laundry, Lidia made her way toward the upper deck, where she was to join Agent Wills and his "wife." Agent Howell was already with them. "Any luck?" he asked Lidia as he moved an empty deck chair near his.

With a grin, Lidia handed him the laundry ticket. "I think he is in on it," read the scribbling on its backside.

"Good work," Warren Howell smiled. "Why don't you all… enjoy the sun." He wanted to say, "Keep up the good work," but that could be overheard by the waiter who was circling the area to pass out refreshments. "I'll see you later," he waved, and with that he left to go to the captain's quarters.

"Mr. and Mrs. Wills" were still engaged in a lively conversation with the Swiss ladies when they saw Lidia and Warren. "It was very nice to have met you," they said, and with a quick wave goodbye, left to join Lidia.

"This could be something important," Agent Wills began as the threesome made their way toward the Bistro. It was almost lunchtime and they had promised to meet up with the other threesome: Adelheid, Viktor and Foster.

CHAPTER 43

The Fortuna was nearing its next port of call and there was a lot of work ahead for the agents. They had to find Gino's, a tavern most likely. Perhaps not so much a tourist attraction but a hangout for the locals. In any case, they had to find it, preferably *before* Leonardo got there. He, as Nancy could decipher from his phone conversation, was to meet with someone at Gino's. But when? At what time?

"Do you think he might recognize you?" Warren asked Lidia after she revealed the plan for her disguise. She was to join him in the search for Gino's.

"Not even you will recognize me," she smiled. "By the way, what time are we supposed to meet at the Captain's quarters?" she asked while glancing at her wristwatch.

"Not until after dinner," Agent Howell informed her.

"Good," Lidia smiled. "I'll see you there."

Once in her cabin, she opened the wardrobe to sort through some clothes. One by one she held up each item while looking in the full-length mirror attached to the inside of the wardrobe door. She wanted to wear something "daring." Perhaps that black lace blouse. But no. When she removed it from her luggage she noticed a button missing. After repeatedly holding up various items of clothing, she finally opted for a navy-blue chiffon dress. *Why stand out in a crowd?* she thought, deciding against the idea of looking daring. A flower-print silk scarf to be worn over a blonde wig completed her attire, except for the navy-blue pumps she usually wore with that dress. High heels wouldn't do on the cobblestone streets often found in old European towns. So, a pair of open-toed sandals was the choice.

A camera disguised as a purse and her bracelet recorder were laid out on the dresser. There was still time to take a little nap before she and Agent Howell were to leave—but not before they had another meeting with the rest of the group in the Captain's quarters.

Lidia had an idea. A "dress rehearsal," she called it, so she purposely waited until past the arranged time of their meeting. Then, with the exaggerated movements of a diva, she entered the captain's domain. Everyone was present. The captain rose from his chair before realizing that this was not Lidia as they had expected. The person before them was a stranger. "May I help you?" the captain asked, a little startled.

"Agent Lidia Frattera at your service," Lidia smiled, taking off her sunglasses and the blonde wig, which covered her raven-black hair.

"You certainly had *us* fooled," the others agreed.

"Shall we begin?" the captain suggested, with a slight urgency in his voice. He had a lot to take care of before the debarkation began. There were shore passes to be signed, radio messages to be answered, and entries written into the ship's logbook.

CHAPTER 44

The meeting with the captain lasted longer than usual. Everyone had their turn speaking, telling of their observations and what they thought might be useful.

The "husband and wife" team told of their acquaintance with the Swiss sisters—what one of them had observed in the middle of the night: two men in swimming trunks, even though the pool was closed. "When she first made mention of it, it didn't seem important," Agent Wills reported. "But we decided to return to where they were sitting, and ever so casually brought the conversation to where it had ended earlier."

"Good work," Agent Howell commented.

"Mrs. Wills" now continued their report. "It's nice of the captain to have the crew use the pool—even if it is in the middle of the night," she said, telling how she had started to chat with the ladies.

"Go on," the Captain encouraged her.

"Well," she went on, "I asked her if it was possible that the two men might have seen her, but she was certain they felt alone because they were using profanity. And even though it was in a subdued voice, it was still audible because the wind came from their direction."

Agent Howell now spoke, "Do I dare ask if she quoted any of it to you?" "Indeed she did."

"And even though it was in Italian, she understood most of it—being Swiss and all," Agent Wills joined in.

"Well?" Agent Howell asked impatiently.

The agent looked around the room. "Excuse me, ladies—but I'm only quoting. These are not my words," he began.

"The sisters had translated the words into English, but we're not sure if they had the same meaning." Agent Wills reached for a piece of paper in his shirt pocket and began to read: "Let them find the d—thing, it's—"

"No." The other man argued, "It's too god—risky, let's just throw it overboard, then we...."

Agent Wills folded the piece of paper to return it to his shirt pocket. "I'm afraid that's all I could find without arousing any suspicion as to why I wanted to know."

"That's quite all right," Agent Howell commented. "You did all right—for a rookie." He laughed then looked at the other female agent who came aboard as agent Wills' wife. "Are you learning anything, Mrs. Wills?" he joked.

"Yes, sir!" came the answer from a rather young "Mrs. Wills." Agent Helen Gandri was new in the spy business; this was her very first assignment.

"Ahem," the Captain began to speak. "Has anyone else anything to report?" His eyes scanned the room.

Adelheid raised her hand. "This lady—did she say where she saw those men? I mean, were they *in* the pool or—just near the pool?"

Agent Wills looked at Adelheid. "You know, now that you ask—they weren't even near the pool because she—I mean the Swiss lady—pointed toward the aft section, where the lifeboats were stored, and then...."

Adelheid interrupted the agent. "I think I know just where to look for what we are searching." She smiled triumphantly.

Captain Demarco rose from his chair. With extended arms he walked towards Adelheid. "Madam, eh—I mean Ms. Adelheid, I don't know how to thank you, because I think you are right. It has got to be in one of those lifeboats!"

Everyone in the room knew what the captain and Adelheid were talking about. It was the elusive printing device they had been searching for all this time.

"Unless of course..." Agent Howell began, "unless they decided to ditch it, throw it overboard, never to be found again"

"Well, we shall soon find out," the captain joined in, dialing a number on his phone. "This is Captain Demarco. Can you get me Mr. Cretin, please?"

"Mr. Cretin is my Chief of Security," he explained, while covering the mouthpiece of his phone.

"Hello, Chief," he began. "Can you stop by my quarters for a moment? We need to discuss something...."

CHAPTER 45

*L*eonardo was nervous, and it was showing. Something was on his mind and it wasn't laundry. "I'll be going ashore tonight," he informed the laundry crew. "Would you let the night shift know? Just in case they need to reach me," he added.

"Where will they find you?" Sophia asked, knowing full well where he was going. She knew from previous cruises that there was only one place where he, Leonardo, could be found: Gino's. No sooner did he depart from the laundry when Nancy Riggs did the same. Sophia and Leni knew beforehand and so were not surprised by her hurried departure.

"Just tell the rest of the crew that I fell ill," Nancy instructed them. She too had an assignment ashore. Like Lidia, she was to use a camera, only this one was a real one, like those all tourists have hanging around their necks. Lidia's was disguised as a purse, or rather, installed in her purse. Nancy's camera had a zoom lens that could see faraway subjects. It also came with a wide-angle lens, which can pick up the surroundings to its left as well as the right. This way, one can take pictures of certain subject, namely Leonardo, without pointing the camera directly at him.

Needless to say, Nancy was also in disguise. Her hair was completely covered by a scarf that was wrapped in a way that it became a turban. Her eyes, shaded by over-sized dark glasses—at least while there was still daylight—completed her disguise. By sundown she planned to be back on the ship again, where she would turn her bathroom into a darkroom to develop the exposed film from her camera in a portable lab kit.

In the meantime, Lidia was getting ready for her role. After the meeting she returned to her cabin to add a few more items to her attire. A pair of earrings and a small brooch to hold together the silk scarf that kept sliding off her shoulders. One quick adjustment, and—oops! One of her earrings got caught up in the scarf and fell to the floor. Clip-ons, rather than those for pierced ears. Lidia scanned the carpet, but—no sight of the earring. She tilted the heavy stuffed chair to search beneath it. And there it was, her earring and something else. A piece of paper. It was the paper that fell out of the brochures on the first day. She had completely forgotten about it. She picked it up. It was blank on one side, but when she turned it over she almost dropped the chair on her foot.

What she held in her hand was a twenty-dollar note but with only one side printed. Andrew Jackson was staring right at her. But the face looked different. It was almost like a double image, as if it were printed twice on the same piece of paper, with the second image off center. It must have been a test-print that for some reason was carelessly used as a bookmark in the brochure and then forgotten. But how did it get in here to Lidia's cabin? Supposedly it was cabin number twenty-four that was being used as a hideout. She would have to figure this out later, she decided, for a knock on the door announced Agent Howell.

"We've got to get going," he urged. "If we see Leonardo leave the ship, we just follow him."

Lidia did not answer. Instead, she handed him the piece of paper. "Where did you get this?" he asked while letting loose a few swear words.

"I'll tell you on the way," Lidia answered as she turned the key in her cabin door.

CHAPTER 46

$\mathscr{H}$enry Cretin, Chief of Security on the Fortuna, was a big man. Burly and muscular—proof of his daily trips to the ship's gym, where he made use of the exercise equipment. In his former life he was a sailor in the U.S. Navy. After his discharge, he studied law enforcement at a police academy, and from there worked his way up to police chief in a small town in upstate New York. He missed the ocean, though, and was hoping to find employment elsewhere where the ocean was nearby. Then one day a flyer arrived in the department's mail announcing job opportunities for people with a background in law enforcement to work as security officers on a cruise line. An Italian cruise line.

Henry jumped at the opportunity and soon found himself on the Fortuna in charge of security. This mostly involved routine walks on the decks' perimeters, checking off-limits areas for prohibited activities, which usually took place at night by passengers who, after having partied a little too much, got lost and perhaps decided to sleep it off in one of the deck chairs, only to discover the chairs had been stored away for the night.

Then there was the danger of passengers actually falling overboard, especially if the alcohol they consumed refused to stay in their stomach. Leaning too far over the railing—well, it had happened before.

Then of course there were the lifeboats. Though they were suspended beneath an overhang, there were rumors that rendezvous sometimes ended up inside one of them. By all accounts, then, it was an easy job for Henry. He was happy and it showed. His jovial demeanor was contagious, and the captain was happy with his choice.

"Come in, Henry," the captain greeted him when he heard the knock on his door. It was time to divulge to the chief what had taken place. The captain had deliberately kept silent about the matter, but now that it was clear who was involved in the counterfeit scam, there was no need to keep things from the chief any longer.

"Why those bastards!" Henry was enraged. "Wait 'til I get my hands on them!" he hissed. "I'll—I'll—" he searched for words to express his intentions.

The captain raised his hand. "No Henry—you won't do anything with them. The Secret Service Agents are the ones who are in charge now. Let them put 'em away in handcuffs and turn them over to the proper authorities"

"So—where do I fit in?" Henry wanted to know, disappointment showing in his voice.

"You, my friend," the captain rose to pat Henry's shoulders, "you are going to find the evidence."

CHAPTER 47

The plaza near the waterfront was buzzing with people. There were several ships that had dropped anchor this Saturday night. Small and mid-sized cargo ships had also moored in the harbor to let their crews spend the night ashore. The locals were out to spend the evening watching ships coming and going, and the vendors and panhandlers were, as in every town near the waterfront, trying to rid tourists of their money.

The local police were out in full force, too, for there were pickpockets and purse-snatchers hanging around whenever a cruise ship arrived, which explained why there were signs posted in multiple languages cautioning unsuspecting tourists to watch their belongings.

The gangplank of the Fortuna was down and passengers were lining up to set foot on land one more time before the ship returned home. Crewmembers whose turn it was to receive a shore pass also gathered off to the side. Once all the passengers had debarked, it was their turn to leave.

This was a good thing, for now the agents Warren Howell and Lidia, as well as Nancy, could debark and mingle with the crowds on the plaza without ever losing sight of Leonardo, who was, as they could observe from a distance, anxiously waiting his turn to leave the ship. He wore a blazer, which was odd since the exterior thermometer read 28° Celsius—more than 80° Fahrenheit. "Here he comes," Howell alerted

Lidia, who was busy trying to ward off a panhandler. The agents' ploy was going to be easier than they had anticipated. The plaza bordered a row of Mediterranean-style buildings and houses with white stucco walls, bright red roof tiles and arched entryways. Eventually, the agents noticed that one of the structures was different from the rest—it had a front yard that reached to the edge of the road. Out front were tables and chairs shaded with big umbrellas on which breweries and distilleries advertised their products.

Had it been dark enough, they would have also noticed the big neon sign attached to its roof. But it was early in the evening with the sun blazing down and reflecting off the shiny metal sign that spelled out "Gino's Taverna."

Leonardo was now on the plaza. One last look towards the Fortuna assured him that none of his fellow crewmembers were headed in the direction he was about to take. His gait was somewhat hurried and his hands kept patting the outside of his jacket, as if to feel for the contents of his pocket.

The agents had a plan. After discovering the Gino's Taverna sign, they would arrive there *before* Leonardo. The opportunity for this arose when Leonardo was accosted by a vendor dangling "precious" mother-of-pearl rosaries in front of him. "No, grazie," the agents could hear their quarry say repeatedly as he tried to convince the poor vendor that he was not religious.

The agents had reached the beer garden in front of Gino's, but opted to find a table inside. It was not likely that Leonardo would conduct his business, of whatever nature, out in the open where he might be spied upon by those in close proximity. After Howell and Lidia each ordered a drink it wasn't long before Leonardo's arrival. The agents had chosen a table near the only other one occupied by a single person, a man in his forties and a local, judging from his attire. This was a good sign. In Italy, locals don't usually sit alone in a tavern. They sit with their friends and neighbors. This could only mean that the man would likely be joined by someone else, and soon.

The agents' speculation proved correct. Leonardo, who was no stranger to Gino's, walked without hesitation toward the man's table. A quick handshake accompanied by some small talk ensued, quickly followed by a barely audible conversation that put the two agents on guard.

"You got your recorder on?" Howell asked Lidia.

"You bet I do," she smiled back. In order to the give the appearance of a couple out on a date, she reached over the table to hold hands with her partner. Warren Howell, a little startled at first, quickly caught on. To make the situation look even more realistic he leaned over and planted a kiss on her cheek. Now it was Lidia who was startled. But this was no time to feel flattered. She knew it was a game they were playing—a game that was part of their job. So no real feelings there. Surely, Howell must have a wife and kids back in the States.

Lidia's purse camera was lying on one of the empty chairs next to her. A casual reach for it had activated the other recorder in case the bracelet-recorder ran out of tape. Before she returned it to its place on the chair, she opened the purse to expose what appeared to be a mirror attached to the inside of the flap. Most evening purses are equipped with such gadgets—built in mirrors, small loops to hold a lipstick and sometimes coin dispensers.

A quick glance pretending to adjust a couple strands of hair on her blonde wig assured Lidia that the man sitting across from Leonardo was in her view finder mirror. The decorative design on the outside of the flap cleverly disguised the small lens of the built-in camera. A faint click obscured by Lidia's throat clearing indicated that the camera was capturing the images they'd come for, catching the face of the man being handed a large envelop that Leonardo had retrieved from the inside of his blazer.

Immediately, Leonardo rid himself of the jacket, hanging it over the back of his chair. By now his face was covered with beads of perspiration, which he wiped away repeatedly with a napkin. He had barely touched the glass of beer in front of him when he rose to his feet, grasped his coat, and with a quick glance around the room, reached for the plastic shopping bag on the chair beside him. With a leisurely show he hung it over his left wrist and covered it with his jacket, then reached his right hand across the table to shake the other man's hand. "Ciao, amigo," he smiled at the man. And with that he left the taverna.

The agents were not prepared for what happened next. They knew that only the local police could make an arrest. But counterfeit American money was involved, which gave them, the Secret Service, the necessary power to have the crooks extradited. Two men wearing civilian clothes got up from a table nearby. With a few words they surrounded the man Leonardo met while showing him their badges. Then, while one of them handcuffed the startled patron, the other reached for the envelope that had earlier been handed to him by Leonardo. A quick look assured the agent that it contained what they had expected. He then turned around to face Howell and Lidia, who had risen from their chairs as had a few other patrons.

"Agent Howell?" the man asked. Before Howell could answer, the other man introduced himself.

"I am Inspector Gradi, and this," he pointed toward his companion, "is Detective Delmonico. We were informed by your Italian contingent what could possibly happen tonight," he began in English that had a trace of an Irish accent. "We knew of you two, and that you," he pointed at Lidia, "would be wearing a blond wig. Besides, your partner," he looked at Howell, who was towering over the rather short man, "well, they told us 'he is tall, and she is blonde.'" He laughed aloud.

The other detective had already left the taverna with the handcuffed man beside him. They'd gone through the back door. Outside an unmarked police car was awaiting them. The driver, in casual civilian clothes, looked at the handcuffed man. He had recognized him as someone who was no stranger to the local police. A second police car was parked nearby.

"I am to take you to the station," Inspector Gradi informed the agents, who already knew that if an arrest were made they were to go to the local police headquarters.

Once there, they were led to a rather small room that could only accommodate a few people—a suspect or a prisoner and a couple of detectives. A ceiling fan churned at its highest speed, but even so, with the room now filling with people, the fan barely made a dent in the heat. There were no windows either and the air was humid and smoke-filled. The few chairs were already occupied as minute-by-minute the room became what Lidia dubbed "a torture chamber." Howell was fanning his face with a sheet of paper that he had torn off a notepad laying on a small table.

"Will you catch me if I faint?" Lidia asked him with a forced smile. Before Howell could answer, the door opened and a uniformed man stuck his head in. "The Chief wants you all to move to the conference room," he declared. A sigh of relief could be heard. One-by-one they filed into the room. There was a table the length of the room with chairs on both sides. This was where the shift change took place, with a uniform inspection usually followed by a briefing on arrests or other pending business. After all had been seated, the Chief entered the room with Captain Demarco and Chief Henry Cretin beside him. After a brief introduction, he asked everyone to state their name and their part in this particular sting.

CHAPTER 49

*N*ancy Riggs was having fun. Well, almost. She was to watch for Leonardo leaving the tavern, then follow him to wherever else he might go, or whoever else he might meet with. So far the only contact made by the suspect was with a peddler selling rosaries. She knew there had been more than one other person that he spoke with on the phone. She had a hunch that it was another sea-to-shore connection. Only during this call Leonardo spoke in a dialect. She could make out the words "dinero" and "moneda," which both refer to money.

Coincidence? Nancy didn't think so. It had to be somehow connected with the phony money. She passed on the information to Lidia, who'd come to the laundry ostensibly to drop off some clothes but mostly to gather evidence that could prove Leonardo's involvement. But how, they had yet to find out. Leonardo was still at Gino's. He had to emerge sooner or later, Nancy figured, so she decided to sit on one of those tables in the beer garden and wait. He's shown up sooner than she had expected, his blazer now hanging over his arm. While walking through the beer garden toward the road, he stopped at one of the tables to chat with some men, most likely just locals who knew him from his previous visits. But he seemed hurried and declined their invitation to a glass of Chianti.

Nancy was right behind him. She had hoped that none of the waiters would notice her; she didn't want to order anything only to have to leave it unfinished, or untouched. She was lucky. The waiter never saw her, or perhaps was too busy to take her order.

Leonardo reached the street. A quick look to both sides assured him that it was safe to cross; it was Saturday night and the road was closed to traffic after six o'clock. Only the residents living in the houses along the road were permitted to drive through here. The plaza was now swarming with people and Nancy had a hard time keeping up with Leonardo. It seemed as if he was returning to the Fortuna. But just before he arrived at the bottom of the gangplank, he changed directions and took aim at a nearby phone booth. It was occupied by someone when Leonardo approached, a woman, who soon left. Much to Nancy's surprise, Leonardo did not enter the phone booth. Instead, he just stood there trying to look casual, although he radiated a certain uneasiness and tension. Still hanging over his arm was the blazer, which seemed peculiar to Nancy since there was no need for it.

What is he waiting for? she began to wonder. She decided to walk past the phone booth, pivoting while holding the camera to her eyes, as if to search for a subject worthy of capturing on film. With her eyes pressed against the viewfinder, she noticed someone new entering the phone booth. Immediately, she swung around to get Leonardo into view. She could tell that this is what he'd been waiting for. Nancy had to back up a little so she could have both men in her viewfinder. "Click" and again "click" went the camera.

"Now what?" Nancy was trying to piece together what exactly was taking place—Leonardo goes to the phone booth, but does not enter. Instead, he just stands around and waits.

Then another man enters the booth. But does he make a phone call? Nancy did not let him out of her sight. With the camera still up to her eyes, she watched his movements.

Another man was approaching the phone booth to wait his turn. Leonardo quickly jumped into action when he noticed the interloper's intent; clearly Leonard did not want this person to enter the booth before *he* had his turn. Nancy had a hunch. The reason Leonardo didn't enter the booth once the woman left was because he wanted someone else to enter it before him. This "someone else" was now in the booth. Nancy watched the man dial a number, though she was certain he never deposited a coin to activate the phone.

"So that's it! This has got to be a drop-off," she figured. "This is getting interesting," she smiled , "just like in the movies, where a person is instructed to drop off ransom money." Suddenly, she noticed the man in the booth reaching behind the post to which the phone was mounted. She could not see his hands, but from what she did observe she got the feeling he was trying to hide something. No sooner did his hand emerge than he placed the phone in its cradle. He turned to face Leonardo, who by now was nervously pacing in front of the booth, never more than a few steps away. The door to the booth opened. Without even looking at Leonardo, the man left and Leonardo took his place. He too began to dial a number—without depositing a coin.

Nancy knew exactly what was going to happen next. While pretending to speak into the mouthpiece, Leonardo lowered his arm with the blazer still hanging over behind the post. Nancy could see what seemed to be a small package quickly stowed away in one of the pockets of the blazer.

He hung up the phone and headed out the door straight for the Fortuna.

Nancy had seen enough. She turned around, aware that her disguise was minimal. Her hair was covered by a scarf and her eyes behind over-sized sunglasses that by now were no longer a protection from the sun, which had already set. The plaza was now lit with huge floodlights. When she looked back, Leonardo was already climbing the gangplank of the ship. Her mission was accomplished.

CHAPTER 50

Foster Morrison was sitting on one of the benches that lined the lower deck leading to the gangplank. In his shirt pocket was a walkie-talkie. The captain had given it to him, as well as one to Viktor and Adelheid so they could communicate with each other once they had taken up their positions.

Foster was to watch for Leonardo's return, a task that could very well last into the night, since there was no telling how long Leonardo might remain on shore. Once he returned, Foster was to alert Adelheid and Viktor, who each had taken up positions in an area they knew Leonardo had to pass to get to the crew's quarters.

At this point, no one really knew exactly what was to be accomplished by keeping Leonardo under surveillance. All anyone knew was that whatever he was involved in was shady. Was he in cahoots with Salvi and Toni? Or was he having his own little clandestine venture? Then there was Maria, Salvi's girlfriend who'd mysteriously disappeared until her body was recovered from the sea....

Which one of the three—Leonardo, Toni, or Salvi—had anything to do with her demise? Not Salvi. He had accused his brother but then had believed him when he swore that he had nothing to do with it. That left Leonardo. What did Foster know about him? There was a person nearing the gangplank. A crewmember posted on top had recognized

Leonardo. "Back so soon?" he asked with a smile. Leonardo responded in a low voice, making it impossible for Foster to hear his answer.

"I'm sorry to hear that," the man replied. Before he could say anymore, Leonardo was gone. Foster almost forgot what he was supposed to do next—alert Adelheid and Viktor. Could he speak on the walkie-talkie without being overheard by the man at the gangplank? To be on the safe side, he left his position to walk just far enough away so as not to be heard.

Foster decided to have a little fun with his walkie-talkie. "Oh Adelheid, I love you dearly!" He began to sing into the receiver.

Adelheid almost fell off her chair when the voice came over the radio. She'd dozed off; it was way past her bedtime. She fidgeted for the switch on the gadget in her hand. "What?" she asked, holding back a yawn.

"Adelheid, dear," the voice again began, "can you hear me?" Foster did not need to use the codename he'd given her. She'd recognize the British accent. "Yes, Foster dear—ahem—I mean, ah—Papa Bear, I can hear you loud and clear," she giggled into the mouthpiece.

"Ahem," another voice came over the speaker.

"This is—Vik—I mean this is Father-Bear—the Lunar has landed," he continued. "Over – and – and – out!"

Instead of taking the stairs to the lower deck where the crew's quarters were located, The Lunar, a.k.a. Leonardo, had taken the rather long walk around the aft of the ship. It was there that Viktor got sight of him. Not another soul was nearby. This was not a part of the ship where passengers ventured. A sign tangling from a chain reading "Authorized Personnel Only" must have assured Leonardo that he'd be alone. There was a retractable ladder attached to the overhang to which the lifeboats were attached. Casually, he climbed the ladder. He wore his blazer now, so he could use both hands to climb the rungs. The plastic bag he'd gotten from the man in the tavern hung on the wrist of his left arm, while the right one was extended to loosen the rope of a tarp on one of the lifeboats. Fortuna #8 was painted on its side. With one last look over his shoulder to make sure no one saw him, he lowered the plastic bag and then the package from his pocket into the hull of Fortuna #8.

Viktor had seen enough. He'd performed his duty. His next step was to meet with Foster and Adelheid. He was about to leave when a voice behind him asked, "May I help you, Sir?"

Viktor turned and discovered, to his relief, that the voice belonged to Alfredo, the captain's confidant. Before Alfredo could speak again, Viktor motioned for him to be silent, putting a finger to his lips. He signaled Alfredo to follow him far enough so they could not be heard by anyone, especially not by Leonardo.

"Did you see that?" he whispered.

"I did indeed, Padre," Alfredo replied. And then, "Are you certain he didn't see you?"

Viktor waved off Alfredo's concern. "Not to worry, young man, I'm certain he did not see me. He would have never deposited—whatever it was—into that lifeboat."

But Alfredo wanted to be sure. Even though they had both seen Leonardo leave the area, he wanted to ensure that he wasn't lurking around in some hiding place. "Follow me, sir," he motioned to Viktor, "and—I'll be speaking Italian to you but you just ignore it."

Viktor, although a little confused, nodded and followed Alfredo. "And here, sir," Alfredo began in his native tongue, "are our lifeboats, which we hopefully will never need to use, except for drills." Viktor nodded again and they continued their walk.

"I'm sorry you got lost, sir," Alfredo smiled sheepishly over his clever ploy, "but this is a big ship and it can happen. Someone must have removed the Off Limits sign."

By now they had reached the common area. Alfredo spoke again, but this time he tried out his repertoire of German to explain to Viktor the reason for his little guided tour. Viktor understood completely. Alfredo wanted Leonardo—should he be hiding somewhere—to believe that he was guiding a lost passenger back to the common area. Once there, they parted. Viktor went on his way to Foster's cabin, where he and Adelheid were to meet, while Alfredo proceeded straight to the captain's quarters to report what he and Viktor had observed.

CHAPTER 51

There was no need for the three sleuths to notify the captain. Alfredo had already done so.

"Let's get the chief," the captain instructed Alfredo. "If he is not in his cabin, then he is probably making his rounds." By "rounds" he meant, of course, the nightly routine performed by Chief Cretin, walking the perimeter of each deck to check on activities that might be prohibited.

"Yes, sir," Alfredo replied, hurrying from the captain's quarters. Just then the captain's phone rang. It was Adelheid. "I assume you already know the news?" she began. "Since Alfredo...."

"Yes, Adelheid, indeed I do. Alfredo has already informed me. And by the way—good job everybody. I shall meet with all of you in the morning. But for now, have a pleasant goodnight." He hung up the phone.

"This calls for a toast," he thought out loud; he glanced at the small bar but quickly decided against it. The intercom unit on his desk gave off a short beep. This meant that a message was about to be announced.

"A land-line, sir," a voice on the intercom announced. Calls from a land-line were picked up in the communications room; from there they were transferred to the person for whom they were intended. The captain knew that it had to be the local chief of police.

"We have a suspect in custody and the Secret Service agents have just arrived."

"Excellent!" The captain exclaimed. "We shall be at your station shortly." He'd just hung up the phone when a familiar knock on the door announced Chief Cretin. It was his signature knock: Dum-da-da-dum-dum, dum dum. Before the chief could complete his knocking ritual, the captain opened the door. A finger held to the captain's lips told the chief to be silent. Quickly, he closed the door while the captain went to his wardrobe to exchange his uniform tunic for a blue blazer adorned with an emblem that read "Fortuna."

"We have to meet with the police chief," the captain informed Henry Cretin. "They have made an arrest."

"What about the evidence Alfredo told me about?" the chief asked, a little puzzled. "Shouldn't we retrieve it before it ends up in the water?"

By now there was total darkness outside—a good time to return to the area where Leonardo stashed his goods.

"We have to leave," the captain reminded the chief. "They're waiting for us at the station." He spoke with a sense of urgency. "But I have a solution," he continued, dialing his phone. After a short conversation with Alfredo, he hung up. "Let's go!" He motioned to the chief, and together they left to go ashore.

"Enjoy your evening, sir!" the sailor who managed the gangplank smiled at the two men. Although a little startled by the captain's rather late departure, he did not make too much of it. What did make him wonder, however, was the fact that the ship's security chief was in his company. "That's a first," he smiled to himself. It wasn't too often the captain would go ashore. But whenever he did, he was—at least most of the time—alone. Seeing him in the company of the security chief —that *was* unusual.

"Thank you, Enrico," the captain acknowledged the sailor's greetings, and with that they were on their way.

CHAPTER 52

*A*lfredo was again on a mission. After receiving instructions from the captain, he hurriedly made his way to Foster Morrison's cabin. He knew that the threesome met there after their mission was complete. He was hoping to find them all still there. It was close to midnight and they might have all gone to bed by now. But he was in luck. When Foster opened the door in answer to Alfredo's rather gingerly knock, he smiled. "We were just talking about you," he laughed, but then became more serious when he noticed Alfredo's urgency.

"I have been instructed by the captain," Alfredo began, "to ask for your assistance." He scanned the faces before him to observe their reaction to his request.

"How can we be of help?" Adelheid asked, suppressing a yawn. By now it *really* was past her bedtime. But, sleepy or not, she was more than ever ready for another mission.

"I need you all to stand watch while I retrieve the evidence," Alfredo answered. He meant the packages that Leonardo had deposited in one of the lifeboats.

In unison, the three of them nodded. "Of course we will help you," they all agreed.

"Why, we wouldn't want to quit now!" Viktor assured the young sailor, who wasn't sure if he and his companions were up to it.

265

"You have to be very careful. I wouldn't want you to get into harm's way," he said with some concern. "There is a chance that Leonardo might show up while we are...."

"Not to worry, Alfredo," Viktor assured him, "we are ready for whatever it takes to catch those criminals"

Alfredo was satisfied. "All right. Here is what you will do...."

CHAPTER 53

The meeting at police headquarters went on at great length and a decision was made to meet again the next morning. By then everyone would also know what Alfredo had found in the lifeboat. So far they had established that Leonardo was definitely involved in the money scheme. The man in custody admitted to having supplied the paper that was used to print the money, but he would not divulge his source.

"They will kill me if I talk!" he pleaded. The envelope given to him by Leonardo held two bundles of money. Both consisted of twenty-dollar bills. One bundle held the real bills, his pay-off, while the other contained the phonies, most likely to be passed on to tourists while making change after a sale of some fake Rolex watches. The man was well known to the local police. He had been arrested before for selling phony merchandise. But now, he'd been caught with counterfeit money in his possession, a felony far more severe than peddling phony wristwatches.

CHAPTER 54

The following day turned out to be a busy one for all involved. An unmarked squad car was waiting at the dock to bring the three sleuths, Adelheid, Viktor and Foster to police headquarters, where Agent Howell and Lidia Frattero were already present. Captain Demarco was to arrive momentarily. He, so he told everyone, had to stop at some local merchants to buy some presents. This time the room was equipped with more comfortable chairs, which the chief had instructed some of his men to bring from the adjacent lobby. A tray with a jug of cold lemonade sat in the center of the long table, with disposable cups next to the jug. The captain had arrived, but the packages he'd promised were not in his hands as everyone expected. He'd been shopping for presents he had explained earlier, but....

The police chief entered the room with one of his men who held a notepad in his hands. A tape recorder was already set up on a nearby desk. "Well, who wants to begin?" the chief looked around the room.

"May I suggest," Agent Howell began, "that we have our three helpers tell us what they have accomplished?"

Adelheid began to relate what had happened the night before. Their mission had begun by them surrounding the area where the lifeboats were located. Again they had their walkie-talkies but were only to use them if they were —heaven forbid! —in some sort of danger.

By then it was nearly midnight and the passengers who had gone ashore earlier that evening were slowly returning. Some showed signs of having indulged a little too much in alcoholic libations. Chianti had definitely done its job. The effect was very evident in a few of the passengers who had to be assisted while climbing up the gangplank. Extra sailors were on standby to guide those who were no longer too steady on their feet or to help them find their cabin.

This was not at all interfering with Alfredo's task at hand. On the contrary. all the attention from passengers and crew-members alike was given to those returning. There was a group approaching the gangplank, belting out some newly acquired lyrics of an Italian love song that they had heard in one of those taverns.

"Mio grande, amore," rang through the night, even if somewhat off-key. Alfredo and his three helpers were ready for their mission. The ladder that was earlier used by Leonardo was still in place next to lifeboat #8 rather than having been retracted—a sign that Leonardo intended to use it again, most likely before the night was over. So they had to act fast. What came next, though expected, was still a shock to Alfredo. Not only did he find the packages which Leonardo had stowed away earlier, but also the elusive printer.

A slight whistle came from his lips, accompanied by what sounded like a special selection of Italian swear words. Foster was already by his side, ready to reach for the rather heavy metal gadget. The bag from the man in the tavern and the package from the man in the phone booth were next. Before he replaced the tarp to cover the boat, he took one last look into the hull but it was too dark to see anything.

"Would you like to use my lighter?" Foster offered. Without looking at him, Alfredo bent over to reach for the lighter that Foster had retrieved from his pocket.

"Yes, thank you, sir, that would really help," Alfredo whispered. And help it did. On the opposite end of the lifeboats, partially obstructed by a row of seats, lay an object. The flame of Foster's pipe lighter gave off just enough illumination to reflect off the metal. A metal box, a strongbox. A common household item, used to store valuables. It was too far away to reach, but climbing into the boat was too risky.

"Could I borrow your cane for a moment, sir?" Alfredo asked Foster in a hushed voice. Without hesitation, Foster held his cane high enough for Alfredo to grab it. Alfredo used the curved handle of the cane to hook into the handle of the strongbox. Slowly, he pulled a little at a time. The noise of metal scraping against metal could attract curious onlookers. Alfredo quickly lowered himself from the ladder just in time, for now there was someone approaching. Luckily, it was only another passenger who'd lost his bearings. Having realized his mistake, he turned around to wander back from whence he came. Alfredo and his helpers had completed another successful mission.

CHAPTER 55

"And where did you keep it during the night?" Agent Howell smiled while looking across the table where the three sleuths were seated. Viktor and Foster couldn't help but chuckle over the agent's question.

"Adelheid," Foster grinned, "would you care to speak to this?"

Adelheid was more than ready to comply. After Alfredo had informed them that it was not safe for him to store the evidence because he had to share his quarters with another crewmember, Adelheid offered to take possession of it.

"...and just to make sure it was all in a safe place until morning, I stowed it under my mattress—I mean the bag and the package. The strongbox I hid... in the toilet, and that—that printing machine—I hid at the foot of my bed, covered with a blanket."

There was clapping accompanied by a roar of laughter from the others in the room. "Then of course," Adelheid continued, "I turned it over to you," she finished, looking at the captain.

"It's all locked up in my safe now," Captain Demarco added.

The door opened to the room and a female officer announced a sea-to-shore call for Agent Howell. "I'll transfer it to this phone." She pointed at a phone at a nearby desk. There was silence while Agent Howell spoke with one of the agents who stayed behind on the ship.

"Chief," Agent Howell began after hanging up the phone, "do you have a holding cell in this building?"

"Indeed we do!" the chief answered.

"And could you send a couple of squad cars to the Fortuna? I'm happy to report that we have arrested Leonardo, as well as the two brothers. The agents are waiting to hand them over as soon as your people get there."

Pandemonium broke out. Handshakes were exchanged and congratulations passed on to those involved.

Just then the door opened again and one of the men in uniform stuck his head in to motion to the captain. Immediately, the captain rose from his chair to follow the young man. When he returned, he held a huge bouquet of roses and a neatly wrapped package. The room fell silent as Captain Demarco began to speak.

"I want to express my deepest gratitude to all of you who were instrumental in the capture of these criminals." He scanned the room to acknowledge all of them, and then continued. "I know some of you make a living catching crooks—you, Agent Howell and your team, as well as Agent Lidia Frattera and, of course, your men, Chief—so my respect and admiration to all of you." A slight bow enforced his sentiments.

"But," the captain continued, "we also have amongst us three people who —well, let's just say we couldn't have done it without them." Another round of applause filled the room.

"Foster, my dear old friend," the captain continued as he walked toward the other end of the table where Foster Morrison was seated. He shook his hand. "Here—this is for you, my friend." The parcel changed hands. It was one of the finest specimens of a Meerschaum pipe.

"And for you, Father Viktor," the captain paused while reaching into the breast pocket of his coat to produce an envelope. "This is a lifetime guest-pass to my ship for any future cruises you would like to take." A handshake and more applause.

Lastly the captain turned toward Adelheid. "My dear lady—Adelheid. You are the most amazing woman I have ever met."

"Hear, hear!" they all agreed.

Again the captain reached into his pocket to retrieve another envelope. "You are welcome as my guest on any future cruises you care to take, and..." the captain reached for the bouquet of roses, now lying beside him on the table. "These are for you, Countess von Schleppmeister"

Adelheid was speechless, something that didn't happen to her very often. "How did you know?" she asked, a little startled as he handed her the roses.

"I just knew," the captain smiled. "I just knew."

EPILOGUE

$\mathcal{I}$t was all now in the hands of the Secret Service. An interrogation of the brothers and the laundry foreman produced enough evidence to put them in the slammer for a long time. The two accomplices with whom Leonardo had made contact—well, one was already behind bars, and the one from the phone booth, the supplier of ink, as it turned out, had yet to be found. So were the ones who were their suppliers, who by all accounts were Mafia connected.

But what about Maria? Who was responsible for her demise? There was Roberto, Maria's boyfriend from back home, whom she had thought she spotted on the ship disguised with eyeglasses and a mustache. Did he revenge himself for Maria having dumped him? Or was she heartbroken when she realized that Salvi, her sweetheart, was a criminal? Or was she silenced because she knew too much?

These were matters yet to be resolved. Would anyone ever find out the truth?

ABOUT THE AUTHOR

*E*lisabeth von Berrinberg was born in Würzburg, Germany, and migrated to the United States in 1955 after marrying an American soldier. In addition to raising her daughter, Lorraine, she had a long career as a darkroom technician both in Germany and the United States. She also held various volunteer positions; she worked for the Red Cross and as a captain in the Civil Air Patrol during the Vietnam era.

Ms. von Berrinberg has given numerous presentations on her World War II experience, which prompted her to write her first book, *The City in Flames: A Child's Recollection of World War II in Würzburg, Germany.*

The Jewel Heist and *The Cruise* are the first and second books in *The Adventures of Countess von Schleppmeister* cozy mystery series. Future titles include: *The Missing Madonna, A Culinary Experience, Mystery at the Pearly Gates,* and *The Doppelgänger.*